Other WORLDS

Other Worlds - First published 2024
Paperback ISBN: 978-1-7394028-6-0
eBook ISBN: 978-1-7394028-7-7

Other WORLDS

An Anthology of Diverse Short Fiction

Edited by Dr Sarah Boyd

CONTENTS

Content Warnings

A Tale of Knives and Arrowheads: References to past violence and colonialism.

The World Under White City: Period typical racism, oppression, sex work.

Cane Men: Homophobia, internalised homophobia.

BLIGHT: Societal breakdown, ableism, injury, blood, death, funeral, body horror.

The Shifters of the Hills: Discussions on abortion, absentee fathers, misogyny, ghosts.

Beneath The Rising Sun: Reference to hostage-taking, reference to past civil war, grief, loss.

Fringe Contender: Underground fighting, graphic injury, blood, body/medical horror, sexual content, legal restriction of bodily autonomy

Old Tricks: Prejudice.

Event Horizon: Death, dead bodies, graphic illness, suicide, religious trauma, implied threat of underage sexual coercion, religious appropriation.

The Island of Coloured Fields: General themes of prejudice and bigotry

FOREWORD

When thinking about other worlds, many things come to my mind. Mythology, the afterlife, portals, fantasy, sci-fi, alien planets… All things I love to think about. After all, reading and writing are about other worlds. Every world an author creates is 'other.' Through words, we can armchair travel to all sorts of places, some familiar and some not. Our imaginations are a portal to any world we desire.

When we feel 'other' ourselves, though, it can be incredibly hard. Feeling like you don't belong anywhere can be, well, alienating. We humans need connection as social creatures, even those of us, myself included, who are introverted and drained by interaction. But how do we find connection when it seems nobody else understands? They don't get how you dress, who you like, or what you say. Who you are. For people who feel like that, diving into other worlds can be a source of comfort. I know I devoured sci-fi and fantasy from a young age as I adored how different everything and everyone was in those worlds. Yet, I also loved how you could always find a character who resonated with you or enjoy how everyone was accepted for their differences rather than being alienated.

Thanks to the writers of those worlds, I embraced my otherness. However, it also got me into trouble. Once, I was waiting outside our chemistry lab at school with the rest of the class, when the blonde, beautiful, popular girl (who no doubt had her own problems) spoke to me. 'What did you do last night?' she asked in that tone, the

one that means 'you're weird, and I'm bored, let's
see if I can trip you up and ask you something that
will make me look great and you look like a nerd.'

I smiled and clasped my big binder of notes. It
had the X-Files 'X' lovingly drawn on it, covered
with all my favourite quotes. I calmly replied:
'Aliens abducted me.' I had not planned this
response.

As the words tumbled out of my mouth, my skin
heated up, and my knees went wobbly. The ground
was jelly, and my eyes could not focus on the
asymmetry of the girl's face. What I could tell was
that everyone was now listening to me. All eyes
were on the strange girl clasping the big X-marked
binder.

'You were abducted,' she said.

I decided to double down. 'Yes, by aliens.' I
knew I hadn't. She knew I hadn't (well, I assume
she did). But I decided at that moment to go for it.
Embrace my otherness and be different. So, I
became known as the girl who aliens had abducted.
I didn't mind. Maybe they had. Maybe the aliens
were my crew, my 'Other' gang. I quite liked that
idea; I fit in with them, the aliens. After all, getting
lost in another world is the best escape from reality.

The other worlds conjured in this wonderful
anthology caught us off guard, so fantastically,
creatively different they are. When you leaf through
their pages, make sure to enjoy the sights and
sounds, the smells and tastes, and let yourself live in
a little sliver of otherness for a moment. Enjoy the
forest and its alien trees, the people who might not
look like you and their complex, strange-seeming

lives that are full of familiar signs of love and life.
The islands of ourselves, the unfamiliar seas and
stars, an unexpected friend, an unexpected feeling –
explore it all and embrace the feeling of otherness.
You are not alone here. We are all wonderfully
other in our alien worlds, and we are standing right
beside you.

RHIANNON WOOD - EIC

THE MIDAS SEA
Briar Ripley Page

THE water looked gold out past the cloud ceiling, like beer – or urine. Moira said it was the same water as the grey-black sea Einar was familiar with, just unshaded, exposed to what she called 'the sun.' Everyone off the island knew about the sun, she said. It was the star the whole planet spun around.

Then, of course, she had to explain 'star' and 'planet.' Einar didn't really believe her. He thought it was much more likely that what his parents and his grandparents and the town elders had always told him was true: to leave the shelter of the great cloud was to leave this world behind and enter another. The ocean was made of different stuff there. If you touched it, it would turn you gold like itself.

Moira got exasperated. 'How come I'm not gold, then? I came from out there!'

She'd washed up on the beach the week before, skin several shades of brown darker than Einar's and short hair the colour of ink. Her ragged dress had also been black. There was a large clot of hairy seaweed splayed across the part of her back between her shoulder blades. When she woke up, she'd vomited so much saltwater Einar was astounded she still lived.

'Maybe you only believe you came from the other sea,' suggested Einar. 'Maybe you fell from the upper side of the cloud. No one knows what's on top.'

'I know where I'm from.' Moira made a face. 'It's always dark here. I miss the light.'

'We have light.'

'Not enough.'

Their boat rocked gently on the low grey-black waves. A seagull landed on the bow and fixed them both with its cold little eye. 'Kreee?' it asked.

'How do you explain birds, then?' asked Moira. 'They leave your island and your cloud. They return. They're still the same birds. It must happen all the time.'

'Birds are different.'

The seagull rattled its wings and took off again as Moira shooed it away. 'Fine,' she said. 'Fine. But I have half a mind to steer this boat out until we sail into the sunshine. Just to show you what's what.'

'I'd jump ship. I'd swim to safety.' Einar felt a sudden, sharp pull at the end of his fishing line. 'Hey! First catch of the morning!' He started to reel it in. Whatever had caught the baited hook was heavy, and it pulled back hard. In the end, Moira had to grip him around the waist and brace her boots against the side of the boat, adding her weight to his, for him to bring the fish on board.

They both looked down at it. Gasping, flopping, thrashing, its gills already threaded with blood.

The giant bass shone like a new coin. Its eyes and scales were the colour of beer – or urine.

Einar lunged forward and grabbed it in both arms. Its tail smacked him hard in the face, and he spluttered as he dumped it back into the water. It didn't seem to swim away as much as sink, a silent gold smudge dwindling into the depths.

'Why'd you do that? Perfectly good fish. Just a funny colour.'

Einar gave Moira a look. 'No. He's been beyond, like I told you. We never eat his kind.'

~

Night was falling. The world became darker at night, and more blue. Moira and Einar crowded in close to the candles at Einar's table, in Einar's shack on the beach. Moira cupped her hands around a flame. 'That fish had scales like fire,' she said.

'Eat your stew,' said Einar. 'Don't just pick the mussels out.'

Moira stirred the briny, lumpy mess around in her bowl. 'I will. I'm just remembering home. Off this island, where there's direct sunlight, you can grow all different kinds of vegetables. And you never see vegetables with hair or teeth inside them.' She had received an unpleasant surprise on splitting a root with her spoon earlier and wouldn't let it go.

Einar sighed. 'Everything alive can grow hair and teeth if it wants. That's harmless.'

'That's harmless, but an unusual-looking fish isn't?'

Einar gave her a pointed stare.

'I'm sorry,' Moira said. 'You've taken such good care of me.'

'If I knew how to get you home, I'd help you get there. I don't, so you might just have to learn to enjoy island living. It's not bad, you know. The cloud protects us. Everyone has what he needs.'

'Does he.' Moira smiled. She passed her left index finger through the candle flame so quickly it didn't burn and touched it gently to Einar's cheek.

She moved closer to him on the pitted wooden bench.

'He has everything he needs, and he wants nothing more,' said Einar, and he made sure his body did not brush against hers for the rest of the meal.

~

Einar woke as the morning began to assert itself in weak striations of grey through the shack's barred window. Moira had gone, and at once, he thought he knew where and why. He pulled on his boots and pushed the door open wide. Looked out towards the pier.

Yesterday, there'd been two boats tied there: Einar's sailboat and his smaller rowboat. Today, only the sailboat remained.

He thought he could see the tiny shadow of a boat with a rower inside far, far out on the water, but in the dimness, it might've been a figment of his imagination.

Einar raced to the pier as quickly as the sucking damp sand would let him and took the sailboat in pursuit. The wind was with him; soon, he could see the figure quite well. He could see the edge of the world too, that line where the cloud stopped existing and the water turned to gold. Moira was rowing towards it, slowly but surely, the muscles in her arms twisting and bulging as she worked the oars. She was very strong, Einar realised. He wondered why he hadn't noticed before.

'Moira!' he called.

A lone seagull called back. Moira looked up, her face strained and sweaty, but did not attempt to vocalise. She was dedicating all of her energy to rowing. Beneath the rowboat, Einar thought he saw slivers of undulating, fiery-scaled flesh in the gloomy depths. A sea serpent, perhaps. A hoard of the golden fish following Moira or spiriting her away.

'Moira, please stop!' He wasn't gaining on her as quickly anymore. The wind had turned against him, grown difficult. It wanted him away from the edge of the world, back to the island's safety.

Moira ignored him. Neither the weather nor her body's exhaustion seemed to encourage *her* to turn back. She was so close to gone, a silhouette against the thick yellow light.

Einar shielded his eyes and did his best to follow. What else could he do? The old, familiar salt spray beaded his hair, stuck his clothes to his skin. The alien brightness pecked at him like a thousand seagulls' beaks. Still, he followed.

Moira herself seemed to become brighter as she approached the line where grey-black water became gold, streaked with orange and red this early in the day. The rowboat brightened with her. Her dress was more indigo than black. Her skin glowed where the bone pressed close to the surface. The oars in her hands were reddish-brown, streaked with white veins of salt.

'Please!' Einar was terrified. 'Moira, I won't chase after you if you leave the cloud!' Would she keep her new colours if he brought her back to the island?

Moira stopped for a moment. He thought she smiled. She called something back to him, but the wind bore it away before he could hear what it was. Then she resumed her rowing, and Einar followed until he saw his own colour begin to change. His skin looked like Moira's oars. Each dark hair on his forearms was limned with copper. He felt warm all over, as though close to a fire. The warmth was what made him realise he could go no farther.

The water was gold out past the cloud ceiling, and when Moira brought her boat out upon it, she turned gold, too, suddenly flaring into illumination that made Einar look away. Bright as a sea serpent. A myth.

He didn't look back as he sailed home. Next week, when he went back into town, he'd have to try to get another rowboat.

BRIAR RIPLEY PAGE

Briar Ripley Page is the author of *Corrupted Vessels*, *Body After Body*, *The False Sister*, and some other books. His short fiction has previously appeared in anthologies like *The Book Of Queer Saints* and e-zines like *beestung*. Briar lives in London and can be found at briarripleypage.xyz. A lot of his stories deal with subjective realities, ambivalent feelings, and people who have difficulty understanding one another.

A Tale of Knives and Arrowheads
Chey Rivera

Now that you're old enough to begin your training, it's time your mother and I told you about Hurricane San Felipe. How it killed more than three thousand people in 1928 and left hundreds of thousands homeless. How it destroyed our homes and forests and dismantled our entire systems of life and law. Sugar factories crumbled into rubble. Coffee crops washed away. For two full decades, our people had no running water, no power, no place to buy food, no police, and no government.

We were alone. No one was coming to protect us, to feed us, to build us new homes. We had to figure out how to survive, who to trust. Some families and clans stuck together; other people formed gangs that became chosen families.

But maybe we weren't completely alone. After the storm, something strange happened to our island. The mountains, the ocean, the trees, they felt more alive, almost sentient. To block our enemies' path and prevent bloodshed, forests grew thicker in an instant, and rivers overflowed without rain. We were more connected than ever to the animals, to the earth. We felt the protection of our home island, even as we were at war with each other.

In these dark times, when trust was a matter of life and death, we discovered that the island gifted its people some part of its protective power. This power took the form of a sign that allowed any individual to bind themselves to another person in a promise of protection – an unbreakable spell. It's a sign parents give their children, leaders give their protégées, and lovers give each other.

You have grown to know the sign. Your mother and I have given it to you since babyhood.

I give it to you now: with the index and middle finger of my right hand, I touch the centre of my forehead, my mind – *my skills are yours.*

With the same hand, I touch the palm to the left side of my chest, my heart – *my life is yours.*

It means I trust you with my life, and you can trust me with yours. It means I am forever bound to protect you, the same way our island is bound to protect its people.

You ask if you're old enough to return it now. I say that five years old is still too young to be making eternal promises, and then I smirk and think to myself that, by the time this story is over, you'll think me a hypocrite. Just know, once you make this vow to protect someone else, the island will hold you to it. It will be in your blood, become part of who you are.

My family, *our* family, the Spears, survived the aftermath of San Felipe with archery. Our bows are sacred. They kept us alive. Generation after generation, they continue to keep us alive.

Twenty years after the storm, The Mainland seized control of our government and turned us into another one of its colonies, offering us their second-class citizenship if we were willing to give up our ways of life, the skills that had kept us safe. Some people refused, and among those were the archers. It was then that our family sought refuge among the trees, using our talents to feed those who chose to follow us, away from the tyranny of The Mainland. Together, we threaded the narrow paths in the heart of the forest, built houses in hidden clearings, and learned the secrets of woodlore.

We built a tight community of outlaws – we are archers and hunters, and our friends are sentries, healers, tailors, cooks. We've always understood that we're nothing without our peers. They help us continue the fight to make The Mainland fear the music of our bowstrings. Whenever mainlanders try to cut down our ancient trees to pave their asphalt roads or take forceful possession of the ocean-side homes of local fishermen to build their rental properties – we do all we can to stop them, using the skills our ancestors passed down to us. We don't take their lives, but we take everything else we can from them – food, money, clothes – and we give it to those who need it most. It's not theft; it's justice.

But not everyone shares our views.

Our neighbours from the mountains and the serpentine roads, the Navaja family, used steel to survive. They became deadly blacksmiths, forging knives and machetes, mastering the art of killing – not just animals, but anyone who stood in their way. They call us thieves, and they believe in protecting nothing but themselves.

I was five years old when their leader, Tony Navaja, entered our forest with his daughter Natasha, who was the same age as me.

You exclaim at the mention of their names, as I knew you would. Amused, I gently bid you patience as I go on with the story.

My father had purchased small knives and arrowheads from the Navajas countless times before, but this was the first time Tony Navaja made the delivery himself. People came out of their blue cobblestone houses, hung from tree tops and peeked through palm leaves to get a glimpse of him. Tony was in a plain sleeveless shirt, his chest and back unprotected by the armour-like fighting gear his family is known to wear – a sign he wasn't threatened. Still, the sides of his legs were covered in his signature throwing knives. He was a tall, burly man, but his most ominous feature was the thick scar running along one side of his face. There was a rumour that Tony had gotten that scar in his first machete fight when he was little more than a child. Legend has it that after he killed the man who'd hurt him, he became invincible, and no one would ever be able to draw blood from him again. I now know the myth is not true, but if you ask him, he will laugh and deny my arrows ever touched him.

I stood on my tiptoes to look out the front window when Tony dropped his parcels on our door and called out to my father. He was in his thirties then, but he had the same full head of white hair he has today. The Navajas are known to show their white hair early. I could already see a thin white streak at the top of Natasha's little head. She raised her eyes to the window, and I ducked my head out of view.

'Come with me, boy. Let it be a lesson on how to deal with the Navajas. It'll be your job one day,' my father said. He crossed the door with his bow and arrows hanging from his back. I'd begun my training by then, but being attached to my weapon was another lesson I had yet to learn. Instead, I grabbed a small bag with my best marbles and followed my father out the door with tentative steps.

I don't remember what my father bought from Tony that day, what was so important or so expensive that it merited a delivery from Tony himself, but I remember Natasha's single white streak. It ran across her head in a perfect line, a flat diadem. I remember her smile, a smirk that said, *I know everything*. I remember the way she said my name when we were introduced.

Robin.

Our parents tried to keep us close by while they negotiated, but it was in vain. We drifted away from them and sat on the ground next to the exposed red roots of a Sierra Palm. I let my knees drop to the earth fearlessly. She lowered to her hands and knees carefully, conscious of every movement, her eyes darting around me to track her surroundings. She was like an unsheathed blade, always sharp and ready.

The marbles clinked as I emptied my bag on the ground between us. We were out of our fathers' sight but close enough to hear the tinkling of my mom's wooden wind chimes coming from the back of our house.

'I don't know how to play,' Natasha admitted, to my surprise. Later, I learned that all Navaja children do is train. Knife, machete, axe throwing. Mixed martial arts. Their only goal from the moment they're born is to be better fighters, better killers.

I made a circle on the soft earth with my finger and placed all but two marbles in the centre.

'Here,' I said, after I'd explained the simple rules of the game, 'you can use my lucky one. It will help your aim.'

Natasha smirked then. You and I chuckle now. My words were a testament to how little I knew about her family at the time, despite all the effort my family put into my education. My father used to say I was born with my head in the clouds, far above the canopy of the trees. Suffice to say, if it had been a real game, I'd have lost all my favourite marbles.

Natasha struck the last marble out of the circle when I heard it: the faint rattle and rustle was unmistakable to a Spear. It was a Taikarayá rattler.

You gasp, and I smile, proud that you recognise the snake's name. You know it's common in our forest. A single drop of its venom can induce a night of restorative deep sleep, but a direct bite guarantees a decades-long coma.

I threw my hand back, reaching too late for a bow that wasn't there. Trying to protect Natasha, I stood between her and the Taikarayá, which got me a kick to the inside of my knee. Natasha impaled the snake with her knife before I hit the ground. A swift, perfect throw. Even then, be it knives or marbles, Natasha never missed.

She pulled her knife out of the dead snake and presented me with the body. The handle of my childhood bow is still wrapped in its smooth, hexagonal skin. 'I'm sorry I kicked you,' she said. 'You were blocking my knife.'

I could only stare at her in amazement.

Tony called for Natasha, and we both hurried back to our fathers. The purchase was made, but they'd been arguing because Tony had raised his prices again.

'I know it's your custom to waylay and rob, but if you want quality Navaja steel, you have to pay for it.' Tony shrugged, pocketing my father's money.

'Did you say that to your masters when you begged them to let you sell to outsiders? I knew you were a selfish creature, but I never thought you'd stoop so low as to make deals with The Mainland. For what cheap comforts do you betray your island and waste your family's strength?'

Tony's lips curled in a sneer, his hands hovering above the knives strapped to his thighs. My father held his bow, an arrow nocked. But Tony knew that, when it comes to human beings, the Spears never shoot to kill, and he turned his back on my father.

'Wait,' Natasha turned back to me. 'I still have your marbles.' She handed me the bag, and I noticed the calluses on her palms for the first time. She later told me it was from swinging heavy axes and machetes. 'Thank you for teaching me your game,' she said.

What I did next was born out of ignorance. At that age, I didn't pay much attention to my father's lectures on history and politics or even take my own training seriously. I was always forgetting my bow, and I had no sense of direction. I could parrot how the Navajas' loyalty was to their own family and not their country, but I didn't know what that meant or why it was so unforgivable that they'd done deals with The Mainland. That understanding would come later. That day, I was simply grateful Natasha had saved me, and I was in awe of her and her knives.

I touched the centre of my forehead with the index and middle finger of my right hand, my mind – *my skills are yours.*

Then I placed my palm on the left side of my chest, my heart – *my life is yours.*

Behind me, my father's bow fell to the ground with a quiet thud. I can only imagine what went through his mind. His youngest son pledging his loyalty, and his life, to a Navaja.

For a brief moment, no one spoke. All I could hear were the sounds of the forest. Then came Tony's unrestrained laugh at the way I was embarrassing my family. The little archer who was always getting lost in his own territory formally offering what meagre skills he had.

I laugh now at the way you cover your face with your hands. Your second-hand embarrassment is appreciated, child. It took me a little while, but my skills eventually caught up with those of my peers, as did other aspects of my education.

Natasha's eyes were wide. It was clear that, unlike me, she had some sense of how inappropriate this was. But then she did something that shocked Tony out of his amusement. It's the first and only time I've seen his features contort into something resembling fear.

She returned the sign.

She gave me her mind, her skills, her heart, her life.

On our island, trust is an old, sacred thing. A vow powerful enough to unite two families surviving the same oppression in very different ways.

A vow your mother and I keep every day.

CHEY RIVERA

Chey Rivera (she/her) is a data engineer and emerging writer from Puerto Rico. Her speculative fiction is inspired by medieval legends, her home island's history and, occasionally, by gothic tales. Her work is out now in Prairie Soul Press' flash fiction anthology *The Philosophy of Blue;* in Cosmic Daffodil's *Seven Deadly Sins* issue; and in *Bleeding Hearts Beat Still*, a collection of stories by Haunted Words Press.

You can find Chey on Instagram @readbychey and on Twitter/X @criverawrites.

THE WORLD UNDER WHITE CITY
A.L. Davidson

THE Chicago World's Fair was quite unlike anything most mortal eyes had ever seen. The city itself felt gilded, the flowers seemed almost alien, and the mass of bodies that shifted to and fro overwhelmed the streets for days upon days that summer. Exotic and exciting views spanned the expansive event, and curious patrons experienced wonders beyond their understanding around every corner. It was a monumental moment, decadent and shining with architecture that bordered on royal and wonders that shook the foundations of many lives. And the lights, oh yes, the lights, they illuminated the city of Chicago like a galaxy in bloom.

It was an event that needed to be experienced firsthand, and it was no wonder people travelled from far and wide to see the sights and experience the magnificent menageries that flooded Jackson Park. Dressed in their most fashionable garments, they arrived expectantly on the thriving Illinois soil, ready to witness the modern marvels of technology and the glistening views of the White City in droves. Somehow, standing in the Midway, taking it all in, all men felt equal.

William knew better, though. He knew he would not be allowed to ride that massive glowing wheel and see the city he loved so dearly from so high off the ground without judgement pouring over him like a waterfall. He could not walk with the crowds and see the sights, even in his Sunday best, without harsh gazes falling upon him. He was just a man, but the world looked at him differently, even when it felt so united.

So he'd opted not to see the sights with the crowds and instead followed a rumour he'd heard muttered in the bar late one night. He'd walked the chatter-filled streets of Chicago toward Graceland, toward the grounds saturated with the soulless and the bodies of the bygone. The cemetery was a place he often visited when his mind needed clearing, that much was true, but never for this purpose. He honestly didn't know how the damn thing was allowed to take place right under the noses of the government, the architects, and the watchful eyes of the world. How it remained so secretive. He hadn't been sure what to expect once he arrived, but he'd known which mausoleum to seek out, what to say, how to be.

Now, lying naked atop a much too small bed with a cigarette in between his lips, he took a few seconds to come down from the world-shattering orgasm and ponder the events that led him here. The desperation. The desire. The defeat.

Perhaps most of all, the loneliness.

The automaton next to him feigned exhaustion – just as it was programmed to do – and turned its flickering eyes to the window. His own whiskey-hued gaze turned in that direction, and he took in the views with a clarity that had eluded him until now. The insanity of it all baffled him, and he hadn't the foggiest how it had been erected without the populace knowing. Without the millions of active souls around not realising something was amiss.

Somehow, the enigma known as The Architect had managed to build a tiny, six-street city beneath the cemetery. One shrouded in shadow and warm, soft lightbulbs that offered some semblance of the sun for the populace of automatons designed to please and pleasure. It was all so uncanny. It felt off, as if the glistening glory of the city above him had been stripped away to reveal the muddy copper tones of how the world truly was. Like the flesh had been stripped from everything, and all that remained was the truth, a truth made of copper bones and mechanical wires that ran on steam and electricity.

William pushed himself up and leaned on the open window frame. He looked at the strange facade of civilisation stretching out much farther than he could have ever imagined. The underground city felt flat, as if it had merely been painted onto large pieces of wood and laid against the carved walls of the Earth. It was akin to an interactive production, one the audience could participate in if they dared to step up on the stage. A play put on for the select, curious few who found the proper ticket and cashed it in. The few who felt the need to explore the sides of themselves hidden away from the world above.

If only the master builders above ground knew, if only the generals at the head of the war of the currents knew, if only the populace at large knew that *this* was waiting just below their feet. William felt that the world would end. It would be cataclysmic, and somehow, that made the moment shared between him and the little bronze-coloured automaton all the more special.

It was a moment born of curiosity, of a need to confirm whether his attraction to his coworkers at the bank or the men at the bars was simply fleeting sin or something deeper. And, in the safety of the hidden city that eluded so many, he'd found his answer. What he would do with that knowledge, he didn't know, but sitting on the short, slightly uneven bed and watching a fabricated world of string lights and buzzing electricity move by at a slow pace, he realised he didn't need to know. Not now.

Below him, ladies dressed in fine outfits chatted with beautiful automatons in the safety of a wide-open bar. Unthreatened by men, by the way the world viewed them, and free to simply exist for once in their lives, they smiled with genuine expressions and twinkles in their eyes. Down the hall, he could hear the sounds of people having sex. Men in the embraces of male automatons, women exploring the feeling of familiar-shaped bodies, discovering that rapturous moment of freedom, of expression, of honesty.

Down here, in a hidden grid of alleyways locked away beneath dirt and death, below the heavenly, pure White City, people could be authentic. It was odd when William compared himself to the faces of those who lived there. The metal bodies and uncanny sense that the bots were more human than they let on. The automatons who resided beneath the soil felt more like kin than his own family, and he wasn't used to feeling so raw, so authentic with another person. If they could even be called people. His thoughts did nothing but wander.

Tinny piano music echoed into the night, and from the ceiling above him – close enough to touch if he extended his hand *just* enough – he could see the soil trickle out of the wooden slats that held it all aloft. As if a heavy enough breath could topple it all.

William took another drag of his cigarette and turned his eyes back to the expectant bot offering up its services to him. Its slightly chilled fingers touched his bare leg, and it sheepishly pulled the thin sheet over its lap.

'What is it like?' the bot inquired of him.

'Pardon?' William asked.

'What is it like? Up there? Where the people are?'

William swallowed hard, nearly choking on the sudden rush of tobacco that saturated his lungs and throat. He hadn't thought of that. Hadn't given these machines the luxury of proper contemplation, of his time. He'd been too overwhelmed by the thought of finally allowing himself to be freely queer, to be freely himself, and the moment he'd laid eyes on the copper-coloured humanoid figure, he could no longer think clearly enough to offer it kindness. But now he pondered the same question himself.

What *was* it like up there? Among the people, under the glistening starlight that graced the city in the form of Edison bulbs and sparkling smiles? This place, its *people*, were not meant to be seen by the masses, to walk the Midway and see the sights. These automatons were not exotic things brought from far-off lands, delicious foods to taste, or thrills to be experienced; they were designed to be held and used by a select few for a select purpose. He hadn't considered whether this place would remain when the Exhibition was swept away like an autumnal wind come October, hadn't considered what the infamous Architect who created this tiny world and its robotic citizens would do when Chicago calmed itself again.

Worse still, he hadn't considered that the automaton before him with the curious-looking eyes and soft voice box hadn't ever seen anything beyond the boxy building that stood as a testament to sex and booze and curiosity at its most raw. Most primal. This little world felt so alien from his own, as if it were his very soul – a soul that felt so lost and confused – untethered from his mortal coil and given substance in the form of wood, paint and wires. The underground city was a reflection of himself, to the innermost core of who he was.

'Busy. Loud,' William finally said after some contemplation.

'I hear the lights are…' The bot contemplated the word it wanted to say. 'Beautiful.'

'I suppose they are,' William replied as he finished off his cigarette.

He leaned his head out the window and exhaled the smoke into the wood and earth.

Below him, a robotic barbershop quartet sang a hymn that warbled in pitch atop a porch adorned with signs of freedom, with ribbons of red and white and powerful blues. The perfectly creased flags felt like lies. How could *this* be freedom? How could this be the only way? How could people like him be relegated to the underground, to the land of the dead, if they wanted to feel worthy? Loved? How could a creator who crafted such beautiful things shun them to the darkness? And why did he see so much of himself in that lost little robot's face?

He didn't know. He could contemplate it for an eternity, but even if he came to a conclusion, it wouldn't matter. It wouldn't change anything.

He watched the fabricated city move with a sort of rhythmic sense of life. The automatons all stepped in unison, like little soldiers marching through a tight corridor designed to resemble a street. The air was a bit heavy so far below the surface, inducing a deathly haze in the minds of the patrons who mingled with the residents. The heavy, arousal-laden breaths felt synthetic, and nothing was quite as real as the nice coats of paint would lead one to believe.

The sound of laughter lingered. It soaked into the wood slats and created a sense of harmony and happiness that felt so unfamiliar to him. Emphasised by the pleasured moans and creaks of robotic bodies, the city under Graceland was one designed to satisfy. To lie. To offer up a slice of perfection, acceptance and understanding that would never again be experienced by those who took the rickety invention called an elevator back up to the mausoleum doors and out into the humid summer air. Back out into the Chicago they knew and loved, one bloated by entertainment and tourism that did not love them in return.

And William found himself wishing this fairytale would last. Wishing the automaton at his side was covered in flesh and filled with thumping arteries. That the satisfaction, perfection, acceptance and understanding would become normal in his existence. That the false god called The Architect, unseen and omniscient, would offer his grace and allow this Eden of the Midwest to thrive. Allow its gates to stay open. Allow him freedom from the judgement of the world that did not accept him for those he loved and desired, the colour of his skin and the manner in which he held himself.

'Did they give you a name?' William asked the automaton.

The bot slid off the bed to go about its protocol and clean itself for the next guest.

'No,' it replied.

'Would you like one?'

The automaton looked back at him for a moment before it grabbed a semi-stained cloth from the side of a wash basin in the corner. It wiped its body clean of the fluids that ran down its plating and pondered. Finding an acceptable answer to his inquiry proved difficult with its limited processing power.

'Am I allowed one?' it inquired.

'We're all allowed to have a name, whether they want us to or not. Do you like the name Robert?' William asked.

'I do.'

'Then, we'll call you Robert. Would you like to see the White City, Robert?'

William slid out of bed and began dressing himself. After pulling his slacks back on and tucking in his undershirt, he took his white button-up and helped Robert slip it over its short arms. The garment was much too big for its small, slender frame, and it hung down below its now-limp robotic genitalia, offering up a semblance of privacy and censorship that William realised it may never have been offered.

It was an intimate moment of connection for them both. For the automaton, it was a kindness it had not experienced. For the human, it was a gesture he had never offered to another in his lifetime. A tender one shared between lovers, something sacred that required lowered defences.

William smiled and extended his arm for the automaton to take. It wrapped its metal limb around him and followed him out into the hall. The short flight of stairs to the lower portion of the brothel groaned beneath their weight, but the sound was lost among the symphony of satisfaction that lingered in the building. The patrons did not turn to acknowledge them, and the automatons continued their programming. Frozen as if to prepare for a photo, the world did not move quickly enough to notice them slip out into the thin street. Did not notice them walk down the rows of makeshift buildings to the elevator that sat firmly between wooden frames coated with so many wires and doodads and sprockets that William couldn't believe it hadn't caught fire yet.

They stepped inside the elevator, and the ornate gate that covered the entrance framed them like a photo. Not in shimmering hues of gold but faded notes of copper. Soft, earthen colours that reminded William of fire, of a sunset, of the falling leaves on the pathways in the park and of the little automaton who held onto his arm like a frightened child. Rich colours that felt warm, felt like home.

As they ascended, the elevator creaked and groaned, and William could feel his lungs begin to fill with proper air. He peered up into the heavens, into the open ceiling of the gravity-defying box that lifted him from the ground like the walking dead rising from his grave, and he could smell the heavy fragrances of soil, of fire and life.

The mausoleum stood quiet, a monument to the mourning it represented, and as the automaton walked across the stone and out into the world for the first time, the sound of its feet echoed like fireworks exploding in the night sky.

William let its arm slip from his own, severing the connection of hope and understanding with a soft motion, and let the bot wander out into the night for a moment without him at its side. Even from this distance, from miles away, the lights of the Exhibition glistened. Setting the horizon line ablaze with electricity and starlight, the White City burned. And burned. And burned. And with its fires came change, change William had to believe would make a difference as nations and worlds became united on the expanse of the city he called home. Something *had* to change. Something had to happen to make his feelings valid, make his existence valid, so that he and the automaton who looked at him with wonder in its fabricated eyes did not have to live in the shadows any longer.

'It's beautiful,' Robert noted with a timid voice.

And all William could do in return was smile, though his eyes were not fixated on the sights, on the grandeur and wonder of a world at his doorstep. No, William's eyes were drawn to the automaton, to the only one who understood him. He took his own first timid step out into the world after this powerful, life-changing night of self-discovery and joined his strange, otherworldly companion in the quiet of the cemetery.

'It truly is.'

A.L DAVIDSON

A.L. Davidson (she/they) is a disabled, queer author who specializes in cozy genre-blending web novels and tales of haunting horror romance. She writes stories about ghosts, grief, isolation, space exploration, disability rep, eco-horror, queerness, and the human condition. They have penned several short stories that have been featured in various lit mags and anthologies, and is a 2023 Indie Ink, Queer Indie, Pushcart Prize, and BBNYA nominee. Their books include *When The Rain Begins To Burn*, *The Scientist, The Spaceman, and The Stars Between Them*, and their collection of web novels—*The Wayward Souls of Avalon*, *Lonely Planet Hotel*, and *The Night Farm*. They are also known for their short story series *R-PNZL: A Futuristic Fairytale*. She is a crazy plant parent and lives with her cat, Jukebox, in Kansas City.

CANE MEN
Roxane Llanque

To Felix Goerdeler
Thank you for your friendship, your vivacity,
and the colour you bring into this world.

NOT many human foreigners found their way to Mandi Bahauddin. The sole example Khalid had ever encountered in the flesh was a very British traveller whose watery blue eyes widened when he saw Khalid and his father's men standing in their twenty acres of sugar cane fields, safe in the shadow of the gaudy tractor towering over them. A metal canvas painted with a hundred testaments to wealth.

The British man was the opposite of their tractor: pale and seemingly devoted to an absolute lack of colour on his person save for his burned, red skin. He stepped forward and asked what on earth this was, with that self-evident English expectation that they would understand him.

Under the confused looks of his men, Khalid answered his impudence with pride: this was his father's tractor, he told him, the backbone of their prosperity.

'This... thing?'

'There is no stronger tractor in the world.'

'You built this?'

'It hails from Belarus.'

Patiently, Khalid explained to the blinking man how Belarusians had brought their metal giants to

Afghanistan in the seventies to sweeten the Soviet pot – before they bitterly invaded Kabul. He told him how the Mujahedeen fought back and seized the tractors, ultimately smuggling them into Pakistan, where his own grandfather became one of the first sugar cane farmers of Punjab to call one of the mighty machines his own. It was the tractors that had made their farming profitable and his family rich – their motor so powerful you could lay the entire crop on a trailer attached to it, and it would still glide through the mud like water, delivering it safely to the refineries.

Khalid looked to their farm in the distance, knowing his father was sitting on its veranda that very moment, sipping his chai and watching his men work under his son, the champion rider. He also saw the British man's blue eyes jump from his men's black beards and strong shoulders to the abandon of colour adorning their tractor: the golden gear stick between painted peacock feathers, the red ribbons lining the doors with a myriad of blue bells, the reliefs of horses adorning the inside walls. Their tractor was the only one so far to sport them – of course, that had been Asim's idea.

Clearly this man, however, could not align the spectacle before him with his no-doubt-important ideas. He bluntly asked Khalid why the vehicle looked like 'something straight from a pride parade.'

Khalid found his pulse quicken in a frightfully familiar pattern at the implication, all the while pushing out his broad chest. He knew that men in Western countries feared colourfulness and adornment. That they were afraid if they and their things looked too pretty, people would think them eunuchs or that three-letter word only whispered in Mandi Bahauddin.

No, this man could not conceive the pride of the sugar cane fields. Nor that different kinds of pride could disguise unthinkable shame to more than one world.

For while this man protected himself with cool hues of nothingness, Khalid-Qadeer was camouflaged by the boisterous magnificence of his father's treasure. For who would suspect the three-letter word of the son of a tractor owner, the glorious leftover of a Soviet invasion? A man who could load that tractor with barrels of sugar cane singlehandedly? A man who could gallop a horse with a pole in his hand like a knight in the sugar lords' horse races fought out by their sons?

But Khalid realised that this man just might; he lacked the proper upbringing to be deceived by his well-honed shield. So, politely and in his deepest voice, he invited him to the afternoon's tent-pegging match in the fields of Dhoul Ranjha. He deposited him on the daybed next to his father's, called the finest musicians of the hurdle to play around them, and swung himself into his horse's saddle, draped in the colours of their tractor.

Khalid's pants and shirt were of a pristine white, the only subdued shade as far as the eye could see. But his and his teammates' crisp waistcoats and turbans were of a shimmering sky-blue – he'd had them changed after Asim had enriched the frames of their tractor's windows with a thousand ombre mosaics of the same hue.

Khalid often wondered if Asim had noticed that. Sometimes, he wished he would – other times, he woke up in the middle of the night with sweat running down the trembling muscles of his back and had to marshal all the powers of his will to keep from running to their stables and ripping their tale-telling uniforms to shreds.

Now, under the suspicious blue eyes of the traveller, Khalid spurred on his horse hung with riches and led his men towards the battle for the wooden pegs with a roaring scream, the white on them splattered with mud under the scorching Punjab sun.

After their victory, he stood before the pleased eyes of his father and the traveller, drenched in mud and sweat, blood running from the scratch on his cheek from where another son had grazed him with his pole. As his father congratulated him, he carefully watched the traveller: he knew the man still hadn't got the faintest clue of the sport, the decorations, the gold and bells on the men, their horses and their tractors. But the new colours on Khalid were clearly something he approved of, the mud and blood reconciling Khalid as a man to him.

His father, oblivious to the test, waved his son down to kiss his cheek. But as soon as the sugar lord was veiled from the stranger by Khalid's face, he whispered in his ear: 'Zahoor has commissioned a new artisan for reliefs in his tractor… his are painted. Go wash up, drive the tractor to Asim and tell him to paint ours in gold.'

So, dutifully, with his heart beating through his chest, Khalid rode his tired steed back to their farm and their tractor. He did not wash up. He climbed from the saddle into the driver's seat and, under the familiar roar and rattle, drove their tractor to the artisans of Mandi Bahauddin. He reasoned that if the mud and blood had fooled the traveller, perhaps they could shield him from Asim's eyes, too, that their depths and dark, which he always feared, could absorb his armour of colour.

When he brought the tractor to a halt next to Asim's house, the young man was kneeling between pieces of sheet metal in his yard, painting sharp-petalled flowers onto them with steady hands. Hands that never seemed to tremble, no matter how long his hours or how strong the wind blowing through the market town. Khalid stood before him with his arms crossed over his sky-blue vest, but the artisan finished his flower with no hurry at all before he finally looked up to him.

As ever, Khalid felt a pang through his heart when he did.

Asim stood and shook out his legs, the top button of his black tunic falling open in the process. Khalid forced his eyes from the artisan's glistening chest to his face; unlike most men in Mandi Bahauddin, Asim did not sport a full beard but simply a well-trimmed moustache, accentuating his bowed lips. Those lips curved into a slow smile as the artisan's eyes wandered over the state of Khalid, finally stopping at the wound on his cheek. 'That needs tending to,' he told him softly. His voice, like his hands, was always steady. Khalid could not remember a single occasion he had ever heard it raised – not even when they had been boys, watching the pegging matches of their fathers.

'It's nothing. Masood was never a good loser – I won't give him the satisfaction of running to a doctor.'

Asim merely studied him for a moment. 'I heard you won again. Why has your father hurried you to me after such a victory? Are the new window frames not to his satisfaction?'

'They are. It's Zahoor's tractor. Apparently, he hired a man out of town to sculpt him reliefs too... his are painted.'

Asim snorted and went to fetch a rag. While he swiped it over his wet neck and the exposed skin of his chest, Khalid kept his eyes level on a button of his tunic.

'I find the white of the reliefs brings out the colours of the counter. What is your father's wish for them, then?'

'He wishes them to be coated in gold.'

Displeasure flashed through Asim's eyes then before he lowered his gaze. 'I do not think that a fitting combination. But of course, your father's wish is my command. Come in, then, and choose a finish that pleases you.'

Arms still wrapped tightly around himself, Khalid followed Asim into his house. The walls could not be seen – every centimetre was crammed with old and new tractor metal, sketches of designs, and meters and meters of colourful cloth and ribbons. Khalid moved through the chaos as if he had a finely tuned compass in his head. He crouched before a glass box filled with bells and pulled forth a wooden chest containing what looked like golden paper in different shades. Without rising, he turned on his heels and presented it to Khalid, who desperately wished the artisan would return to his eye level.

'Is that paint?'

'No. It is plated gold. I recommend the white one, but choose what pleases you.'

Sweat running over Khalid's temples, he carefully shifted through the different sheets, all the while painfully aware of Asim's dark eyes on him. Carefully, he pulled the white-hued one on top. 'I trust your expertise,' he managed to mumble.

Asim merely nodded and went to work immediately. After climbing into the tractor, he fastened the sheets to his reliefs with such gentle and confident care that Khalid could barely stand to watch. Asim's work often seemed a little like magic to him. The artisan began to brush over the sheets until they started to dissolve, their gold moving to coat the running horses Asim had so lovingly crafted a month ago.

When it was done, Asim asked to accompany Khalid to his father's, eager to hear if his work was satisfactory. Khalid did not think a man had ever driven one of the tractors with such iron focus as he had, the artisan sitting so close to him, his head turned towards the window and his hands absent-mindedly caressing his artwork on the tractor's interior. But his tunnel vision fell apart when he parked the tractor in front of his father's house and saw the blue-eyed man sitting beside him on the veranda.

While his father basically jumped over Khalid's lap in his eagerness to inspect Asim's work, Khalid saw the traveller shake his head at the new gold with smug amusement.

'Oh good, more gay glitter,' he muttered under his breath.

His father, barely knowing the English tongue, turned back to his spiteful guest with a proud smile. 'Yes, it is glittering, isn't it? The best glittering tractor in Pakistan.'

Khalid balled his fists then and finally allowed the anger he'd contained so carefully to spill into his mind. With a breath so sharp it hurt his chest, he tried to remember that this man was not capable of appreciating a tractor. To him, sugar came out of packages or glass shakers. Sugar labour would be if he ever attempted to powder a cake by himself. To him, Belarus was bad, and nothing good could come from it – or nothing good that wasn't better elsewhere. To him, prideful colour and love of detail on men was something to belittle... something to be feared.

'Do you want to take it for a spin?' he heard himself asking.

The man's smug smile wavered. 'What?'

His father hissed at him, told him no one but their people was allowed to even get near the keys. Khalid continued to pin the traveller with an unblinking stare.

'Can't you?'

'Um. Of course I can drive.'

'A tractor?'

'...Well, I... I never exactly had the chance.'

An uncomfortable silence followed, the traveller shifting on the muddy earth and his father looking between them in incomprehension. Finally, Asim cleared his throat and asked the sugar lord if the coating was to his liking. Khalid's father first blinked, then laughed and enthusiastically patted Asim's cheek, praising his work and pressing a handful of pressed bills into his hands. Then his father jumped out of his pride and joy and put a hand on the traveller's shoulder, ushering him to a celebratory dinner. The blue eyes diligently evaded Khalid's dark ones until they disappeared inside.

Khalid stood there staring after them until the sound of the passenger door opening made him startle.

'I can walk home,' Asim announced softly.

Kahlid turned around and looked into the gentle eyes, unsettled, trying to recall how it was that they were here. Then, with a determination that surprised him, he climbed back into the tractor. 'No. I'll drive you.'

Asim was silent through their brief ride to the artisan quarters. Khalid's thoughts, though, were loud. He found himself wondering what the thoughts of the Mujahedeen were when they first laid eyes on the enormous tractors brought by the Soviets. Were they afraid? Did they think they were weapons? Had any of them imagined they would become the most beautiful and desirable thing to behold in the eyes of every sugar cane farmer in Punjab?

Asim had to put a hand on his arm when Khalid drove past his house. Khalid cleared his throat and hit the brakes sharply. When the motor died with some coughing, the silence of the night suddenly became deafening to him, and he feared that Asim could hear his heartbeat disrupting the whisper of the cane around them.

Asim had not removed his hand from his arm. And when it climbed up and finally cupped his heated cheek, Khalid pressed his eyes closed at the tenderness of the touch.

'May I tend to your wound?' Asim asked softly.

Khalid, feeling wide open under the artisan's hand, could do nothing but nod.

And Asim let his hand glide down to close around his, leading them home.

ROXANE LLANQUE

Roxane Llanque is a German-Bolivian writer, artist, and filmmaker. Her award-winning short film *Aberration* was selected for The Madrid Human Rights Festival and her micro *The Tell-Tale Present* won the 2023 Outstanding Miniature of World Pride Australia. Her writing was featured in the anthologies *We Are All Thieves of Somebody's Future, Demons & Death Drops*, and is forthcoming in the sci-fi anthology *Not Your Papi's Utopia: Latinx Visions of Radical Hope*. She is currently working on her first novel. You can find her on her website https://roxanellanque.com or on social media @roxanellanque

BLIGHT

Samir Sirk Morató

THERE is illness in the wind and unease in the soil. It has been here since 1904 when the first splotch of chestnut blight showed in our hills; it will be here until the last American Chestnut is dead. The trees fought hard, but their oak and pine neighbours haven't hidden them, and their lapfuls of saplings die young. Once the cankers show, it's over. The era of 500-year-old elder groves has passed. We now live in a graveyard of toddlers.

The chestnuts are dead. Not silent. We hear them crying behind pelt-tacked sheds, around foreclosed mines and closing food pantries, behind holler-claimed houses. They cry in the night; they cry at the dawn. No land is bereft of them, no hour left unwept.

Despite our own blights, we've tried to help the chestnuts. Why wouldn't we? They fed us in the cold and shaded us from heat. We burnt, bent and harvested their cradle-to-grave bodies for years, but out of love; we needed them. They wanted us.

Much has changed.

~

Every time Bessie Swanson sees her daughter, she tells her:

The trees are crying.

Maybe to remind her where she's from. Maybe because she herself forgets. Through it all – the flood, the fleeing after, the pitying scholarship, the funeral (Bessie's divorce) – if they're speaking,

Harper says, *I know, Mom.* It's always disbelieving, only sometimes condescending.

This time, with her door locks broken and back hurting, Bessie can't say it. She wrings her arthritic hands. Fidgets in her rocking chair. Flies skitter across the fresh zucchini on the counter. Who's sneaking in and leaving those horrible vegetables? It's evil. It's indecent. Bessie mutters, *When I recall her, there'll be hell to pay.*

Harper, belly swollen, fingers ringless, picks at the tied curtains before giving her a concerned look. *Who cut down your chestnut trees, Mom?*

Bessie licks chapped lips. Did she have something to say? There's a blank, blank space, a nothing; ringing the nothing is fear. She fumbles with the third stale bagel stacked in her pocket. Her eyes water.

What trees?

~

Angel. Stop fucking with me.

No, Sis, I'm serious. I didn't touch anything. The lawnmower was gone when I got back. I found it wrecked in the ditch.

With the keys still on the hook.

If I was going wild again, do you think I'd do such a pisspoor job?

Sissy rubs her face. The cousins stand before the ancient sawmill, boots caked in mud, calloused fingers blooming from fingerless gloves, both of them in Sissy's coats, one of them at ease in its shape, the other more uncertain. A dead hillside of chestnut trees looms.

Dad's going to flip his shit, Sissy says. *Especially with you just out of rehab.*

Angel's exhale wavers. Her eyeliner draws bottomless gouges around her eyes. *You don't have to say anything. You've stuck your neck out enough for me. If he doesn't believe me, I'll take the blame. I need to show him I'm trying.*

He knows you are. You know.

Rainfall seeps downhill, washing mineral sores left from mining as it goes. The land gurgles. The girls shuffle. Exchange a cigarette and uncertain smiles. One of them kicks the lawnmower wheel by her toe. They avoid discussing where the trees were – where the trees are.

Neither of them follows the torn, oil-flecked trail past the sawmill into the woods.

~

I ain't arguing with a dumb bitch that don't know what a punnet square or p-value is. Trees don't cry or walk. They don't do no 'talking' outside of chain chemical reactions. The government and agriculture folks done spent millions more on saving those trees instead of us, and you know what? Even they *don't believe them damn chestnuts can think!*

You should finish driving back to Morgantown.

And what, leave your schizophrenic ass with our mother? I bet you've been using her morphine patches. Her vitamins too. That's why they're gone.

That's why you've got homoeopathic bullshit on the brain.

Get in your damn truck, Eddie.

I'm drunk. Can't drive.

You're the one getting a PhD. Fucking figure it out.

Headlights splash against bark in a bright pulse of blood, an engine roars, a duffel slaps grass. The Elk River and all its mineral-soaked streams rush by, hurrying towards all the open roots, mouths and wells that await it. In the trailer, a woman made of pain is wailing. One of her sons – the younger one, eternal caretaker until tonight – stands in the drive, his nails biting into his palms. He watches his older brother swerve through their mother's garden, crushing unpicked tomatoes and trellises. Squashes explode under his tyres. Unripe chestnut burrs explode.

The teal truck straightens, then roars across the bridge.

~

Where's the bird?

What?

Rusty Senior, hooked to an oxygen tank and wheezing, stays in his chair. Rusty Junior, still in his sawdusted uniform, walks to their drooping clothesline. He squeezes a weathered sock hanging from it. He frowns. Curls of wood stick in his lashes and kinky hair; the moss beneath his boots squishes. Their family bustles inside.

The wren, Rusty Junior says. He turns the empty sock in gentle, saw-clipped fingers. He and his father are too young for all they're missing. *She hasn't been sleeping in the sock anymore. Shouldn't she have eggs this time of year too?*

Something must've got her.

They stare into the darkening field. The twilight-striped wood beyond the road. It's a bone thicket to Rusty Junior. A grove of dried loss. He wants to say, *Maybe she finally left this shithole,* because no one's come to fix the house after the flood like they've promised, no one's assessed anything, no one's ever come for them, but the wren's always eaten worms delivered on bent wire, raised her babies in potted peppers, and slept in a laundered sock. They've made it good for her.

Something's screaming in the hills like a baby slid out of it half-done.

Must've been the trees, Rusty Senior says.

They lock the door that night.

~

Jillian's mascara is running, sweatshirt and bun melting off her, while Reese huddles in his varsity jacket. The friends sit in silence, sniffling as Jillian whips them around curves in the darkness, her inherited car groaning, crumbling beneath them.

It makes me so sad.

Jillian speaks. Stares ahead. Reese's gleaming paper clip braces and the gaps between teeth, absences of gleam, vanish. Cross after cross and guardrail-tied bouquet after bouquet slide through the headlights.

You can't stand in line anywhere without hearing about someone sick or dying. Everywhere. Every day. In two seconds, great-auntie went from talking about her stolen mulch to that lump eating her stomach. Your uncle told you about his lungs in the stupid Kum & Go.

Reese says, *I think it's normal.*

They corkscrew down the mountain road, needling into its exposed granite side, asphalt and stale deer blood paving the way. Jillian wipes her nose.

My parents won't even talk about my uncles since Eddie got the DUI and Theo got arrested in Charleston. Especially Theo. They only talk about Eddie now that he's getting a degree. Theo's the one taking care of Auntie Zora, and they pretend he doesn't exist. I don't know how they're gonna handle Auntie being housebound with Theo. I really don't.

Reese, remembering the middle school era when Zora's house was a forbidden plague place, chews on his tongue. He can't articulate what his and Jillian's mental heaviness is beyond birds flying north for winter, woods walking, or a river flowing backwards. It's unnatural. He recalls Theo's wan, crumpling face when Jillian's parents – more present and loving than his own – made them shun Theo in a Dollar General.

He can't look at the idea that he and Jillian are next.

They said Theo's name for the first time in years today. Jillian sniffles, face screwing up. *It's like he's dead. It's like we're all dead. Lord, Reese. I have to get out of here. I have to get out.*

...Jilly. It'll be okay. You're not alone. Reese touches her as they round the curve right into a tree-cut pair of headlights.

Right into a tree.

~

That night, we share a dream.

It enters our collective veins the way soot and pain do. We are standing together, dying, begging for the chestnuts' aid. Without axes or baskets, we can't force it. An oily river boils around our shins. Our feet are buried. Sores bloom on our exposed skin. The chestnuts, their faces made from shadowy whorls and peeled trunks, ever-changing illusions, stare at us.

Why? they say.

Do they actually walk, or is it just the wind? Our hard, unfinished children lay scattered on the pine needles.

We've never forgotten you, the trees say. *You've forgotten us.*

We'll do anything to be better, we tell them. We mean it.

Will you?

They watch us rot.

When we wake up, it feels so real, we don't think about it at all.

~

Harper is searching for black dresses when she hears the back door open. She stills, bent in the dim closet. Morning has wrapped the house in fragile, yellow light, but it has yet to bring heat; all that's come is a shredded rabbit in the yard. Summer has not been dying as it should. Harper straightens, slower than before, scribbled lists of maternity supplies and budgeting math rustling in her waitress apron.

Her mother is napping. It must be old Zora, here to deliver vegetables to her sister-in-law. Maybe out of pity or desperation for control. Bessie has long forgotten that she gave Zora friendship or a house key. The head of a shadow creeps beneath the open closet door, then its shoulders. Footsteps and muttering lurch closer. Harper, nose sensitive, catches a whiff of earth. Below it, iron. Concern spikes through her before nausea.

Hello?

A shadow lies across her feet. She closes the door.

Bessie stands a touch away from her, naked, leaf-tangled hair between her shoulder blades, blood on her crooked nose and in her eye, blood streaking sagging breasts, blood on lashed, wrinkly thighs, brown of the earth overwriting the brown of her skin.

They put their dead in me, she says.

Harper screams.

Bessie mumbles as Harper cleans her, nurses her and dresses her. She hunches on her worn loveseat while Harper makes a call, crying.

Rus, I don't know what to do. The lock was broken. Someone beat her. She at least fell into some briars. Can't take her to the hospital or police after everything. What the hell is going on—? Can you? I've known you since high school. I know when you're... Okay. No, I'm all right. Please, please be careful.

Harper cries in the wet-faced, dead-voiced way she always has, but her fingers curl in the landline coil as if tenderly seeking hair. She cradles her belly. Bessie laughs, her nose raw with broken veins and roots.

We ought to be helping, she says. *We ought to have helped them. Now look.*

~

The funeral for Jillian Hyer makes a grove of them.

The community gathers around the coffin, bent together, untouching. Sissy and Angel, who supplied the coffin wood, brood beside the family. They stand hand-in-hand, chins lowered. Their father weeps behind them. The coffin makers, junior and senior, stand nearby. They are intertwined with another family – Harper melds into Rusty's side, one hand on her mother's shoulder.

Reese, whiter than birch, banded with bruises, speaks after the preacher does. His parents don't look at him.

The reverend says death is part of God's plan, Reese says. *Maybe I'm too stupid to follow it. I miss Jilly. I'm in pain. I haven't learned anything at all.*

Words and blame-stench, as sharp as drink, leak beneath Reese's eulogy. Voices rise; a cup flies at the reception table. Two brothers quiet when other mourners turn. The bruised one looks away. Around them, poplars whisper.

I have a warning, Bessie mutters.

Then Jillian's grandaunt Zora, squeezing a bouquet, rises to speak. A revelation lights Bessie's face. She explodes from beneath her daughter's grip.

It's you! she screams. *It's you, you fucking bitch! I remember now! It's you breaking into my house and leaving those zucchinis! Leave me alone!*

The woods weep.

~

Two nights after the funeral, dogs are brought inside. Doors are locked. Labourers leave the woods before sundown. Though there's light and dinner smoke, curtains cover unboarded windows; guns above mantles are loaded. Only whitetail and already-dead drug runners traverse the thin roads that night. Chestnuts rustle. Rattle. *It's windy out there,* those listening say, although the sky is still. The sound of the dying drowns the countryside.

Around the hollers—

An old woman's room lies silent.

Her daughter sleeps with a man, her belly against the small of his back, their dark hands restlessly knitted. The cost of their love echoes in medical bills, union dues and long-spent scrip. They don't want to pay interest.

A family house hums with dim music, doors locked, heads down. They understand hiding from neighbours. It isn't their first time. They always pray it's their last. They fear what the desperate will do.

By the river—

Squash goes unharvested. Condolence meals go uneaten. A woman denied her prescriptions lies shrouded in quilts and baby photos, waiting on her sons to return, praying the bumper dent on one's truck means something else. She (again) resigns to living through this.

Two cousins-turned-sisters drink Irish coffee from teacups. *Fucking party at my funeral!* one howls. *Make them bury me in a dress!*

And the other cries: *I'll outlive you, just to make sure they do.* They pretend their exes are healing and their drinking water is clean.

Near the hills—

A woman screams into her husband's chest, undone homework underfoot. *It should've been me,* she and the trees say. *It should've been me.*

Down the road, a teenager looks at his palms, bed unmade, and wonders (again) if he was born only to die.

In the woods—

Two men stand in clipped briars. One holds a flashlight. The other holds a tree parameter map. Burrs cover their boots. They argue about vanished groves, root holes, guilt, grief, familial mauling and drag marks in undertone until the eldest shouts. He points at a chestnut trunk sliced with teal. *I told you I didn't hit them!* He weeps. *It walked. It walked.*

The youngest doesn't reply. He stares at the ruined figure ambling towards them.

In the graveyard—

fresh soil settles on a ripening girl.

~

You don't know what I did to have you. Do you?

The coat draped over Bessie sways. The brothers steady as her as they slide down the slick hill, furrows of blood and duff behind them. A screech owl shrieks.

We won't have service until the road, Eddie says.

I know. Theo chews his lip. Deer bones clatter against his boots. He stumbles when Bessie seizes his forearm. She digs her heels in.

Harper! One of her breasts, gnarled with burrs beneath the skin, swings free. *You liar! You don't know! Are you listening to me?*

The brothers lock eyes for a breath, debating, before Theo says, *Yes, Mom. I'm listening.*

You should be! You're expecting.

The group creeps forward again. Bessie's raw legs shake.

Would you eat a baby for your baby? she says.

Did you? Theo says.

I ate so many chestnuts. Bessie wheezes. *I sold those coal people my mother's house. I did about everything to have you whole. To not have that horrible crick water and baby bits coming pouring out of me again. It's the mines. They're sick. They kill everything. Well, Harper? What'll you do?*

When Theo's silence stretches, moral childlessness and hereditary nightmares heavy in his face, Bessie slaps him. He yelps in surprise, her blood on his cheek; the waning moon swallows their scuffling.

Harper! Answer me!

Leave him alone! Eddie seizes her hand before she can hit his brother again. *He ain't done anything wrong beyond lying to spare you!*

Bessie trips, plunging into the leaves on her knees, screaming.

Your people blighted the burr people! Then my people and my grandbaby's people. Then the world committed to killing you. Now we're together! Everyone outside doesn't care. The burr people don't care!

Theo gasps when the woods move. Roots tear from the ground, mistletoe-bloated limbs from the canopy.

I think I had something important to say, Bessie says.

~

The chain of phone calls and banging on doors brings us from our homes, but the flashpoint of fear drives it. We converge at the gravel road – young and old, singular and pregnant, pained and able – stuffed into boots and mended camo coats, flashlights shimmering in hand. Everyone lingers at the woods' hem, afraid of its silence, until someone surges forward. Then we plunge into the trees, looking for what they've taken.

At first, we clamber past oaks, ashes, and pawpaws. We fling leaves at toadstools with our boots; we trample moss and rusted barbed wire. Our lights illuminate only raked earth. Then, the woods open. The moonlit truth spills.

We make a terrible discovery: we find what the chestnut trees made.

It's an apothecary of awfulness. We see stews made from our vitamins, cleanses crafted from engine oil and ointments, poultices made from fly-blown fertiliser and ground wren chicks. We smell sap on stolen blades, bleach on the toadstools. The entire blighted chestnut grove, the dead and dying, the fertile and the falling, stand knee-deep in their efforts. Some have roots wrapped around mason jars, cankers doused in cures, or trunks slathered in terrible salve.

Some now bathe in blood.

Bucked-and-limbed human trunk splatters the forest floor. Autumn's colours have come early. Sopping rags hang from bark necks. Iron-dripping fingertips poke from hollow chests. The dying chestnuts stand dressed in three of our generations. Someone moans. Retch splatters black barren vines. Chestnut branches reach for us, breaking through shock and light. The woods close in.

How could you do this? one of our youngest cries. He already knows the answer.

We all do.

SAMIR SIRK MORATÓ

Samir Sirk Morató is a scientist, artist, and flesh heap. They are also a 2022 *Brave New Weird* shortlister and a *F(r)iction Fall 2022* Flash Fiction finalist. Samir spends most of their time tending to their cacti and contemplating the nature of meat.

55

THE SHIFTER OF THE HILLS
Busayo Akinmoju

BEFORE the white men came, the family lived a half-day's journey from the town they belonged to. Up alone in the hills. The smoke of their kitchen fires showed all who hated them down below that the Adeyanjus were still there, alive. Banished. Of the first generation to bite the curse under their teeth.

Every evening before sunset, the family's house was shuttered tight with the blue-grey door the father swore was impenetrable to his two wives and eight children. They could sleep well at night, he promised. Even if the house was weak, makeshift and with a roof that leaked in hard storms, the spirit that wandered in the forest among the hills could not enter – would not enter no matter how hard it tried.

There was no doubting that the spirits existed then; this was before the white men came with a God that cast down demons, when they came with chalky yellow pills that cut down diseases that were curses from the gods. This was before the Adeyanjus were fed fat on a thoroughly logical education, when in just a generation, their old beliefs were disregarded, seen as self-indulgent superstitions.

In the beginning, when they were openly hated, living alone on a taboo of a hill, Yinka woke up at night to see his father's chair moved from its place against the wall – each night closer and closer to the fire. Till the raffia hairs were singed anew every morning. Yinka hoped the banging against the walls, the humming from the windows were spillovers from his dreams. That the chair was moved while he was asleep. By someone human.

It was still early, then, when Yinka woke one night to the smell of burning raffia, and the next morning, his father was gone. Fallen from a palm tree he had been climbing for years.

He stopped waking up at night after it happened. He no longer heard banging against the mud walls. His sleep was always blank, dreamless. And it remained that way till he had his own son.

~

When the white men came, Yinka's teeth were rotted to the back rows from years of chewing tobacco, hazing his mind not to dwell on what lurked or didn't lurk in the hills. It was a wonder to the townspeople that the white men chose him – a man alone, of middling age and with no exceptional skills. His eyes were glazed over half the time, his mind far off and focused on somewhere beyond the hills.

But it was reasonable; a man alone is easy to conquer. All the villagers who watched Yinka's kitchen fires had been united for decades by their desire to hold off any threat, anything that seemed ready to disrupt the peace they had prayed for, had sacrificed whole harvests for. They were impenetrable.

Yinka, with the repeated grief that marked his childhood: first the death of his father, then the disappearance of his mother – off into the forest one day to hunt for mushrooms, never seen again. Only heard on odd nights by her children, singing far away in the forest. And one by one, Yinka's sisters followed the voice as it rang with that singing. And were never heard of again.

When the missionaries came, they found a man more than willing to accept what the gospel promised – a father, a whole family of other people bound in love. A new life.

~

Once, there was a night, and it wants to be remembered this way: boys.

Boys who woke up out of their sleep and whistled into the moonlight. Standing in a circle, their voices created notes like moonthread, weaving a fabric that was part music, part silver and completely power.

When their song ended, the boys glowing with an infinite power, ready to fight in the war threatening their village from all sides, one of the boys was silent. He was running a thought in his mind.

Before sunrise, any of them could sequester all of that power they had sung for, all to himself. He would be invincible, wielding a power that was unmistakably supernatural. If they all shared that power, the sixteen boys, each of them would be as strong as iron, faster than the wind, their voices like storm clouds. But alone with all that power, the person would be able to shapeshift. To make himself into anything that crawled on the earth. From the humble centipede to the lion to any human that existed or had existed.

The silent boy ran that thought over in his mind.

What would it be like to see the faces of his dead family again? One by one – his siblings, his mother with her beautiful smile curving back at him in a pool of water. Even if he couldn't touch them, if he could hear their voices come out of his own throat, if he could stretch his hands out and see the weak fingers of his twin, wouldn't that be worth losing any war for?

Because, even if the village won against the raiders, what would be left for him in this desolate, cold world without the touch of a loved one?

All the boys walked back home, confident of victory. The silent boy walked back with a delicate smile on his face, confident he would see his mother after the sunrise.

~

The rector had a problem.

His parishioners kept seeing things: today, a leopard sitting on a tree in the primary school courtyard; tomorrow, a dead relative of the king with all of the scars to prove it, including the bit of his earlobe that had been cut off during his lifetime. A little girl even saw the late missionary who had converted the first person in the town. But everyone tried hard not to believe her.

The rector had tried very hard to get his brother to stop it.

'Why do you keep doing this, Dele? Why?' he had asked.

And Dele, with all of the brimming annoyance he always carried, responded. 'Please, tell me why not. Why exactly not?'

The rector took off his glasses. The reason *why not* was very clear: he was scaring the people of the town. He was making the town backslide – a people who had been reluctantly persuaded to the faith were seeing signs that they needed the protection of the old ways to hold off the evil that had returned to the town.

And more than anything, the rector thought, he was making the Adeyanju family, who had been even more reluctantly accepted back into the village, suspects.

No one in the town really believed that the leopard was something that had strayed from the forest. The creature hadn't done anything; it just stared intently at passers-by with its white-gold irises. There were people old and alive enough to remember why the Adeyanjus were banished into the hills in the first place.

The rector tried a different approach.

'Do you realise you are putting the family in danger? You have a son, for pity's sake.'

At this, Dele was pensive.

He did have a son, a one-year-old sapling who still had a gummy smile.

But then anger welled up inside of Dele. His brother couldn't understand. He was covered by the halo of the ministry – the basic good faith people had in him because he was the one who doled out blessings and tributes on behalf of the Most High. The rector could never understand that no one else in the family had ever been fully accepted back into the village. They were treated with suspicion.

While the rector had spent his childhood locked away in serenity, being taught in the faith by missionaries who saw good promise in him, Dele and his father had to deal with townspeople who saw only evil in them. Only allowing them back in because they were the extension of the change that was coming to the town – the pills that cured coughs that had lasted for months, the things they did with pen and paper, how if one apprenticed in the study of this pen and paper craft, they could go on into faraway cities, become even bigger than any of the chiefs in the town – and, some whispered, even bigger than the Kabiyesi.

They only let the Adeyanjus in because they were a means to an end.

Dele understood this. He understood it painfully. So why wouldn't he tease or terrorise them when he could?

And besides, it was only mild, what he had done so far. He hadn't turned into a sea monster or killed anyone. He could if he wanted to – he knew the people were slow enough to blame it on some spirit that lurked in the hills.

Dele looked at his brother, half-hearing his pleas.

The spirit in the forest, Dele began to think, hearing a strange and distant music.

~

Yinka's father became an outcast the moment it was sunrise.

It didn't take long for everyone else to realise their super-strength was non-existent. They had their usual skinny or flabby or toned bodies. But none of the powers they had expected.

The culprit was easy to pinpoint: the only one of them who wasn't there. Who was found somewhere off by the riverside staring at the water, a silly smile playing on his lips.

He was dragged to the middle of the market square, his clothes stripped, a confession rushing out of him before the first angry blow struck.

'I did it. I did it. I did it,' he kept saying over and over again. Like a plea, like a prayer.

He should be killed, everyone in the town agreed.

But to kill someone who held such power, no one in the town had ever done so – and who knew what would happen if they tried it? What evil would hover over the town if they destroyed the vessel that carried such power?

Instead, he was banished. For life, for the rest of his bloodline. True to the path Baba Yinka had chosen, each generation would have a son who would be a shapeshifter. But as would happen to Baba Yinka, each father would die a few years after they produced that son.

To cleanse the town of the evil Baba Yinka had brought to them, they sent him into the hills. Gave him the two orphan sisters he had been eyeing for years, and he went off.

He had stolen music from the throats of others; he would go into the hills, and whatever lurking thing that sang there would finish him off soon. The villagers did not believe his bloodline would last more than a generation. He would be silenced by the spirit in the hills before he bore any children.

But it wasn't their business either way. He was gone, only the smoke rising in the mornings showing them that someone better forgotten lived there.

~

It was hard to hear anything over the noise of the speakers, but Kolade didn't need to understand sign language to know what Eunice was trying to say.

The silly girl was pregnant.

She rubbed both hands over her belly, gesticulating. Her lips mouthing the words, 'Na you get am.'

He didn't doubt her. Silly as she was, the girl was a virgin their first time together – he had even seen the blood if he'd dared to disbelieve her shyness.

But this was no simple matter. Kolade was married – estranged from his wife but married still. He hoped to get her back once he got his money sorted out. The nightclub was doing well, it wouldn't take too long. So, a baby from another woman didn't really fit into his plans. Especially since Kolade and his wife had decided thirteen years ago not to have a child. If Kemi found out – the cheating, the jealousy would never allow her to forgive him.

'Follow me,' Kolade said to Eunice, straining his voice over the speakers.

He wove through the writhing bodies that danced through his nightclub. And again, he felt proud that the unwanted ones – the freaks, the deviants, the alternate ones with alternate ways of living their lives, of finding love, of finding community – had a space they could come to and feel among friends. Feel at home.

If Kolade were in the mood after speaking to Eunice, he would transform into an eagle that night. Have the jolly people marvel at the wonder of such a magnificent beast. At how beautiful they could all be too if they let go of what the world prescribed to them. He would let them hold onto his feathers, kiss a bright red eye. Feel a part of the magic too.

These transformations were the open secret that made his club so popular. He still held a hint of bitterness that they were also the reason he'd had to flee from the town of his fathers. For his life.

Still, Kolade was happy he had the life he had. Soon, Kemi would be back with him. He would have more than enough money to take care of her, and Kemi would never have to live with her older sister again.

The baby had to go.

In his office above the nightclub, Kolade pulled out a drawer and counted some money. He held out some crisp notes to her.

'Get rid of it. Commot am,' he said simply.

'Commot am as how? Na your pikin now,' Eunice said in surprise.

'Na my pikin?' Kolade said incredulously.

He tried a different approach.

'How can I know it is even my baby? Silly girl like you, have I not caught you with that AY of a boy? The two of you doing nonsense.'

At this, Eunice fell on her knees.

'Abeg, Broda Kolade, I no get any other person. I no fit run go house with pregnancy.'

She began to cry.

But Kolade was already irritated.

He had given her a solution. A baby was not something either of them could deal with right now. She was nineteen, had some dream or other to go back to school. He had his Kemi to win back. The solution was clear.

'I no fit do abortion. I be child of God,' Eunice said.

Kolade laughed derisively at her. Someone who had so willingly offered herself to him? Calling herself that?

'Child of God. Of course.'

He walked out of the room.

'When you are ready,' he called to her, 'you will take the money and do what needs to be done. I have done my own part.'

Five months later, Kolade was reunited with his wife, sleeping every night in her arms. And he got a telegram. Three short words.

It's a boy.

He sighed when he saw it. Tore the message into tiny pieces. Tore the pieces into even smaller ones. It would soon be over. He doubted the prayers the rector had said over him had worked. Kolade had been advised to leave the town once he was a teenager and began to shapeshift. The town would not tolerate another Adeyanju. And the rector had worked so hard to raise him to be proper – despite Kolade's constant rebellion. It would be easier if

Kolade left. Left the town to a quiet it had forced itself to have.

Soon, Kolade thought, he would go the same way his father had – led into suicide by some strange, mindless music. By the same frustration of not belonging.

Maybe in a year or two, he thought as he shredded the message, he would begin to hear it. Maybe it would even come out of his own speakers at the nightclub. He looked at his wife as she slept on their bed, her abdomen peacefully flat all the years they had been together. He wondered how many they had to go.

The town had won again.

~

'Money no be the only thing wey dey this life,' his mother said to Akintunde over the phone.

He had begun to agree with her. Reluctantly.

The search for his father had upended so many things in his life.

First, his mother – usually open and vivacious even in her sixties – suddenly became withdrawn when he said he wanted to look for his father. The nebulous man whose name – Kolade – had accidentally slipped out of his mother's lips.

Akintunde wanted to find whatever traces of his father were left in the world.

That his father had died when he was six did not mean there would be absolutely nothing left of him. Every man had a lineage – at the very least, he had some place he could trace his ancestors to. He had to find it.

The second thing that happened – after he decided to find his father – was how uncontrollable the urge to shapeshift became. And it was to the oddest things – a random pillow, a pen on his desk, or the red car with the broken wheel he had played with as a child.

Even his mother as a younger woman. Eunice the soft-cheeked.

That particular one – transforming into his mother, into anything in a public bathroom, was ill-timed.

But he had felt that urge right there and then in front of the bathroom mirror. He wanted to see what his mother had looked like when she was with his father. Had she not been beautiful enough, her cheeks not round enough to make him stay?

He had been about to change into the boy he had been – to search into that face and discover what about it a father couldn't love.

Then he heard a snicker from behind him.

The idiot intern had caught him. The boy had been stalking him for weeks since his urges became out of control.

But there was nothing to do now as his face melted back into what it usually was. Everyone had seen it. Plain and out there on Instagram Live.

He walked out of the bathroom. Not saying anything.

Got home. Got drunk. The next day, his phone was ringing off his bedside table when he woke up.

He ignored all the messages and, with a bright-red headache, instructed his assistant to clear up 'the issues.'

Basically, throw money at the problem. As he always did.

As his mother told him would be ineffective. (You couldn't buy out every single blog on the internet.)

Yet hers was the only phone call he picked up.

'Money can't do everything,' she repeated.

He cradled his head in his palm and listened to his mother breathe through the phone —weighing her options, deciding how she could help her very lost son.

Finally, she said, 'If this is what you have decided, your father's people are from Oka. You can find it on your own. But please, just know that they will try to kill you if they find out who you are.'

She prayed for him. He listened patiently. Whispering *Amen* in the right places.

In two hours, he was on his private jet flying to Oka, finally reading through the social media posts that ranged from calling it slick video editing, to unimportant, to the evils of the rich Illuminati people. To calling him a witch or some variant of a thing that did not deserve to be alive.

It had been forty long years of being in the wilderness, he thought once he landed in Oka. The bright green hills were scenic, cradling a small, bored town. His mother had told him about the particular hill that was the abomination. Her father had told her about it one evening when he was depressed about something or the other. Homesick for a place that rejected him.

It was there, just the way his mother had described it. A grey hill with a flat top – he was surprised to see, even far off, that the old house still stood there.

Shouldn't the decades, the rain, the wind have eaten it up?

He shapeshifted into a falcon, flew over the hilltop and looked below. The roof of the house had caved in. An old clothesline with browned bed sheets was still shifting in the breeze. He flew in through the roof and turned into a gecko to get a better feel of the place. Finally, he rested on an old raffia chair.

So this was the place, he thought to himself as he pulled the chair outside.

He sat in the backyard, pulling at the still-singed hairs of the raffia chair. This place felt like a story. But it also felt empty. Like a snail's old shell. Uninhabited. Untouched. Feral.

There was silence. But there was also an odd music in the gentle breeze.

He had come all this way and still felt nothing. Still felt the same gnawing emptiness that had chased him his whole life. He had chased money, had chased accolades. And now, he had tried to chase old ghosts that didn't even want him.

Why was he the way he was? What was the meaning of him being able to turn into anything – and still not want to be himself? Because he didn't even know what that was. What was the answer to the mystery of the whole thing?

Who was he?

The angst that should have died in his teen years, like everyone else's, still lurked.

And here in the old house of his ancestors, nothing waited for him.

He listened again to the quiet emptiness. Watched a white bird call above him.

And in the wind, he heard unmistakably the voice of his mother. *Not empty, my child. It just isn't your turn yet.*

And it might never be.

BUSAYO AKINMOJU

Busayo is a writer. Her work has appeared in *Lucent Dreaming, SmokeLong Quarterly, A Coup of Owls,* and the *Kalahari Review,* among others. She won a category prize in the Welkin Prize for flash fiction and is a Pushcart nominee. She likes to read and to relax on long walks.

BENEATH THE RISING SUN
Victor Okechukwu

THE sun settled at the east. It was July, and rain had not fallen. After the scourging harmattan at the beginning of the year, there had been hopes for heavy rainfall, but those hopes lay shattered on the arid red soil. Nevertheless, they still planted and sought ways to water the soil. The corn seeds had sprouted, sending down taproots and starting to develop their first leaves, but they were still tender. They had to be saved. Miriam plucked off the weeds that surrounded them and tilled the soil around the corn plants to protect them from frost. She held her back and stood upright; the pain was becoming severe. She cleaned the sweat from her brows. *I wish Chigozie was here to help*, she said, the twentieth time. Chigozie knew how to tend the plants better than she did; she hadn't watered them enough, and some of their leaves were shrinking so early.

The noise of a revving engine was drawing close. She walked to the front of the bungalow where Deborah had parked her dirty blue lorry, covered with grease and dust. Crushed insects blackened the silver slash across the grill.

'Any luck this time?'

'Yeah, but the stream is almost dry,' Deborah said, coming down from the lorry. 'I got some cans of water.'

'Enough to water the farm?'

'I'm not sure.'

'And they are still brown in colour?'

'What do you expect?'

Miriam hissed, 'Don't you think it's time you go to Ekwe village to get better water?'

'That's a hell of a journey this lorry can't go through.'

'Seriously? Ekwe is just the next village.'

'It takes more than five hours to get to Ekwe and another six hours to return. And how many hours would I queue at the stream?' She put her hands on her waist. 'We are just a large, empty community that doesn't even have water.'

'Why don't you see any good here?'

'Ekwe isn't as demoralised as we are.'

Miriam mounted the back of the lorry and counted the cans of water. 'Only five?' Ten were empty.

'We aren't the only farmers here. And we left some for another day.'

They had two full tanks of water they used for bathing and cooking but couldn't use on the farm because they weren't sure when the rain would fall again. They poured the five cans of water into the tank that faced the farm and switched on the rain gun sprinkler. They had decided they were going to cultivate the fifty hectares without Chigozie's help, but when they began to suffer chronic back pains, they stopped, cultivating just half the farmland. Miriam gazed in anguish as the water sprinkled the plants and the uncultivated areas. She was relieved and also bitter that they wouldn't have the full yield this year. This was her first experience. Before, it had been Kingsley who made sure the farm was fully cultivated, but Chigozie took over from him when he got ill. Sometimes, Chigozie had invited his friends to come help him, and Miriam would just sit and watch their bodies turn murky gold under the sun.

Deborah, her elder sister, had been of great help, but she couldn't do much because she drove around the community seeking either water or corn seeds. *When will the rain come?* she said. That seemed to have been a perennial question on Miriam's lips since the year began. Some people said that the aftermath of the civil war placed a curse on the Eha-Amufu community. Others believed it was a spiritual problem – many young men and women leaving the community for greener pastures, God punishing their parents for their failures.

She heard a scream from the house. There was a quickening silence everywhere that made the scream echo. What could be the problem? She ran to the house. In the parlour, Deborah gasped and trembled with a white paper in her hand. Miriam collected it. It was a letter from the government. It read: *After several investigations by the police, the Intelligence Team and the Secret Security Team, we have come to believe that the fifty-five passengers who boarded the train from Eha-Amufu to Jos on the fifth of July are presently missing. Suspected bandits planted explosives, which caused the train to stop, after which they took the passengers hostage. N.B. All rumours of death are falsehoods spread by opposition parties against the President, who is working tirelessly to see that all passengers return to their homes safely.*

Chigozie had been a passenger on the train. A week ago, rumour spread that bandits had kidnapped the passengers and demanded ransom from the government, but Miriam doubted it. She had tried calling Chigozie with her Nokia 338, but it never rang. She had heard some of her neighbours say that sometimes it was hard to get hold of someone in the North.

'It's two weeks, and this is all they come up with.' Deborah pointed to the letter.

'Where did you get it from?'

'The mailbox?'

Miriam read it again. Twelve days after the news that the passengers were missing, the government had sent a letter that said: *We call for calm and togetherness as we investigate the incident. We are sure that with your collaboration, all the passengers will be safe home as soon as possible.* She had thrown that letter away because she didn't believe anything it said. But here was another proof. She squeezed the paper and threw it away.

'I'm sorry,' Deborah said, hugging her.

Miriam resented the feeling of pity. She needed faith.

'He's still alive,' she said.

Deborah looked into her eyes; they were moist.

'Maybe… Perhaps the government will see them before they get hurt,' Deborah said.

Miriam sat on the blue couch close to the centre table facing the television and buried her head in her hands. Would she lose another person so dear to her? Kingsley had died of cancer – something understandable – not this talk of Chigozie missing. What if he was already dead? She rejected the thought.

Miriam cherished her deep motherly instinct anytime it came to Chigozie. When Chigozie was six months, he'd had pneumonia for a week and almost died. One night, at midnight, Miriam had woken up and found him struggling to breathe and sweaty. He had cried all day but stopped after she gave him fluids and antibiotics, and she'd thought that he was all right. But seeing him struggle to breathe heightened her fright. He was pale and limp.

She hadn't woken Kingsley up. She'd taken Chigozie and run barefoot to the community hospital three miles away. While running, she had sometimes felt he was dead, but she couldn't let go of her only child. When she got to the hospital, the nurses had quickly given him an antibiotic drip, and then he had a steamy bath.

Miriam could smell the leftover potato porridge Deborah was warming. She wasn't sure if she was hungry, especially after reading the letter. She pondered how difficult things had become over the past few months, from no rain to Chigozie going missing. She sighed heavily and felt very tired.

Deborah served the food in the dining room.

'Aren't you hungry?' she said.

Miriam didn't reply.

Deborah sat down and began to eat. 'Please, come and eat.'

Miriam held her back in pain while she walked to the dining room. She munched slowly without talking and didn't catch Deborah's eyes.

'This community is like a ride on a roller coaster,' Deborah said. 'You can't move. You can't stop. You can't get out. And if you get out, you better stay out because the community is a gamble between life and death.'

Miriam didn't say anything.

'This community is a giant sleeping in its shadows.'

'It's not only the community, it's the country,'' Miriam said, finally deciding to join the conversation.

'Whichever way you put it. They are still the same thing.'

The golden globe of the sun had dispersed into the morning mist in which the atmosphere was veiled, and now its burning shafts radiated on their brown bodies through the rectangular window at the right.

'We need to water the farm tomorrow,' Miriam said.

'Yeah, of course.'

'But the water we got in the tank won't be enough.'

'We don't need to irrigate the farm every day.'

'But the weather is very hot, especially at night when the earth seems like a burning coal.'

'I will see what I can do.'

Miriam finished eating.

'Or we can pray?' Deborah said.

'Let's take prayer out of this.'

'Do you still pray?'

'Sometimes.'

'I didn't ever believe you would stop praying after you began following Kingsley to church.'

'I pray secretly, Deborah.'

Miriam took a short nap in the evening. The pain in her back hadn't reduced. She was tired of farming, tired of waiting for rain and of the frustration at how little the farm would yield this year. Also, the news about Chigozie had made her weak. She sweated in her blue satin gown. The ceiling fan blew a hot breeze. The chirping noise of insects invaded her room. She lay on the bed gazing at the ceiling. The last time she felt this weak and tired was the day Kingsley died – two years ago. After months of struggle with prostate cancer, he gave up the fight. She had forgotten the verse of scripture he always quoted to her each time she cried that he was going to leave her soon. She picked his dog-eared bible up from the table close to the bed. She didn't know where the quote was, but she knew it was in the book of Jeremiah. She flipped through the pages of Jeremiah from chapter one and scrolled down each chapter until she got to chapter twelve of verse five. Verse five was circled with a spot of blue ink. She read: *If thou hast run with footmen, and they wearied thee, then how canst thou contend with horses? And if in the land of peace wherein thou trusted, they wearied thee, then how wilt thou do in the swelling of Jordan?* Tears were already crawling down her cheeks.

'Why do you keep quoting the verse?' she'd once asked.

'It awakens me to fight on.'

'But you still suffer pain.'

'It's part of contending, not trusting in what you have but just the struggle.'

'You always get me confused.'

'If you don't contend, how can you win? And if you are wearied in faith, you are as good as dead.'

Kingsley and Miriam had waited ten years for Chigozie. Kingsley called it 'Ten yearning years.' But those ten yearning years were what had bonded them and helped them live happily. Some women in the community had been surprised by the way Kingsley relied on Miriam for every decision he made.

'I don't know how to take care of myself anymore,' Kingsley had sometimes said to his friend. 'She makes my life so simple for me.'

As farmers, Miriam dictated the prices of their farm products and kept a record of all that went out of the farm. And because they earned so well from selling farm products, Kingsley had fewer worries about how Miriam spent the money. He'd always played with Chigozie, who people said was a 'carbon copy' of him. His small eyes, flat nose, round cheeks and pyramid jaw were the same as Kingsley's. Miriam had been happy she had two Kingsleys in her life, but she loved the junior Kingsley more.

At the latter end of Kingsley's life, he became a faithful Christian. He served as a pulpit usher a year before he was diagnosed with prostate cancer. He never missed The Community Baptist Church activity for any reason. Even when he was very sick, Chigozie and Miriam had rolled him in a wheelchair to church. The bells of the church, the choir hymns, the sanctimonious worship, and the reverend's daily message about an angel having one foot in the sea and another in the land and his right hand raised to heaven – it all made him so happy.

'Father seems to touch the heavens anytime he's in church,' Chigozie once said.

It was amusing to Miriam because it had given her hope that Kingsley was going to survive, at least for her sake. Chigozie had prayed so earnestly for his father that if prayers could save a man from death, he would never have died. But when he did, Chigozie mourned for three days without food; he was more miserable than Miriam.

She walked to the veranda to meet Deborah.

'Do you want some coffee?' Deborah said.

'Yes.'

Deborah poured a cup for her.

'It's really hot inside,' Deborah said.

'Like boiling coals.'

'Rain clouds seem to be gathering with no other sign.'

'Maybe tomorrow morning, the rain will fall.'

'Let's say next tomorrow.'

It didn't take long – a great charge of lightning exploded, striking the humid air with a sinister violence. At once, massive rocks of rain hurled themselves down upon the sleeping earth. The noise was deafening to the ear, the sight awesome to the eye, and the great torrents almost startled them into premature senility. Miriam and Deborah ran into the rain and began to scream for joy. Neighbours ran in the street shouting in ecstasy while some rolled on the muddy road in astonishment; even little children were dancing under the rain. The rude buckets of water poured over their anguished souls. It drummed on the window panes. It dinned in their minds. It drummed down upon them until they couldn't stand it. It poured darkly – plashed, guttered, broke down upon their heads like the smack of a fist. It roared, splashed and stuttered torturously down from the black spaces of the huge, mindless universe. It rose. It swelled. It cracked their sides like a whip.

Deborah and Miriam sat on the floor until the rain stopped. For the first time in a long time, they happily held their hands together.

Miriam woke up before Deborah. She said her prayers and read Jeremiah 12, verse 5. She went outside to feel the energy of the day. The wind blew gently. Peace and tranquillity filled the air. The sky was blue. She smiled. Walking back into the house, she saw the crumpled letter from the government close to the door, picked it up, read it and tore it to shreds. Last night's rain had brought fresh hopes, and she wasn't ready to throw them away for such dispiritedness.

Last year, a group of students travelling from Enugu to Kano to meet their parents hadn't reached their location. The police had declared them missing, and rumour had it that they had already been killed by robbers. But after three days, they suddenly reappeared and said they had met armed robbers on the way, so they'd left their car and run into the bush and stayed there for two days because they were scared to death. That may be the same situation here, Miriam said. Until she saw Chigozie's body, she would never believe anything bad had happened to him.

Deborah hadn't left her room, so Miriam decided to go view the rail-line coast. She had been there twice since Chigozie left. And each time she went there, it reignited the belief that Chigozie was going to come home soon. The rail-line coast was two streets away after Akanu Road, at the rising of the clay hardpack road that sloped down to the railway tracks. When Miriam got down the slope, she met Mr Okoro, the railway manager for thirty years, who was now in his mid-sixties. He was sitting on the red sand. Miriam greeted him and stood at some distance beside him.

'It has always been busy here,' Mr Okoro began, 'but since the forces of evil descended on us, we have been left demoralised.'

'I don't see forces of any kind of evil; I just see an empty rail station.'

'You don't understand.' He shook his head. 'I've managed this station for t-h-i-r-t-y years. And I have seen its highs and its lows, but there has been nothing like this.'

Mr Okoro's jeans were dirty; he had a red cap and a large brown coat on. His brows were wrinkled, and his hands so hairy that they looked almost like goat skin.

'I don't believe it's the civil war that caused it,' Miriam said.

'Then what?'

'Life – chance – time – everything a man can think of.'

'Let me tell you something you may not know too well. This rail line was built in 1914 by J.K. Burroughs and Sons Hydroelectric Engineering Company. We became the centre of trade that linked us to cities like Jos, Zaria, Onitsha, Aba and many others. Traders flocked here like bees in a honeycomb. But all that was swept away by the civil war. The Nigerian army destroyed the rail line so that the Biafra militias wouldn't have any link to other parts of the country. After the war, it was repaired, but guess what? Only a few traders came here. And now, our sons and daughters run to other cities and towns. Look at how everywhere is as still as moss. I pleaded with my boy not to go like the others and that things would improve, but he said he wouldn't end up like me.' He laughed. 'Of course, no one wants to end up a farmer when technology has redefined everything we see and believe. Now, the government is lying that he's lost while he may be dead.'

'Chigozie is still alive.'

'The truth will come hard on us.'

'I accept what I believe.'

'I feel, one morning, I'll tie a rope round my neck and kick the chair away.'

'Why?'

'This is a hopeless community.'

The Baptist Church bell rang. Mr Okoro stood up.

'Aren't you coming for service?'

'No, I got something to do at home,' Miriam said.

'Yeah, I understand.' He chuckled lightly. 'Just that I have only seen you in church a few times since your husband passed away.'

Miriam looked at the wooden cross on top of the church roof.

'Let me go say my dying prayer so that I can meet my maker in peace,' Mr Okoro said.

He walked down the slope.

The wooden cross reminded her of the morning Chigozie left. She had resisted him leaving for four months, but he kept persisting. Deborah made sure she never came into the matter because sometimes it led to quarrels between Miriam and Chigozie.

'The North is dangerous, you know that. Bandits and kidnappers are becoming a threat,' Miriam had said one night while they sat on the veranda.

'I'm a man now,' he said.

'Shut up that dirty mouth of yours,' Miriam said. 'You're too young to go to places you have never been before.' He was twenty-three years old.

'I've got a dream, Mum,' Chigozie said. 'I want to return and build a fine house for you.'

'I never told you I needed a house.'

'You've been through a lot after Dad died, and the only way I want to repay you for being the best mum is by building a new home.'

'Then stay and be my best son.'

'But for two years, the rainfall has been dropping. And it will get worse. Travelling and starting a business in Jos would provide better for us.'

Miriam had shaken her head in disgust. 'A week from now, we will have to start cultivating the farm.'

'We can't keep living on that. Every year, fewer traders come to buy from us, and if we send them to the market, the profit will be worth nothing.'

'That's the only thing I was trained to do.'

'Father always said that, *If in the land of peace wherein thou trusted, they wearied thee, then how wilt thou do in the swelling of Jordan?*' He held her hand. 'All I'm doing is for us. You can't let what people say about the North deprive me of going there. People still live there. There are multimillionaires there – no one has kidnapped or killed them.'

Miriam smiled. Even though she hated the idea of going to the North, she loved his vision of going there. 'I love you so much,' she said.

'I love you too.'

Miriam had kissed him on his forehead.

The morning he left, the station was crowded. Other parents and relations had bid their sons and daughters farewell. The bell of the Baptist Church rang before Chigozie climbed the coach and waved Miriam goodbye. The bell rang like the tintinnabulation of wind chimes blowing in the breeze. She had felt like running to join him, but she gazed up and saw the wooden cross. It reminded her of Kingsley, and she pledged to stay where her lover had died. The belching steam and the slow rumble of the rails had made her heart and body quake. The conductor was shouting, 'Going-to-Jos… Going… Go.'

When she walked down Akanu Road, a few passersby were heading to the church. Women with scarves wrapped around their heads and men with their little bibles in their armpits. This community that was as still as moss came alive when it came to going to church. The aftermath of the civil war had led many to believe in Jesus and His saving Grace. The community reckoned that only the mercies of God could overturn their misery and despondency. After the rain had fallen yesterday, many would pray more, believing that if God could answer them and send rain, he could answer them and deliver their sons and daughters from their prey. Prayer was the key, so prayer became their only resort. But only a few went to pray for their missing children; most of them prayed for death, just like Mr Okoro. But Miriam believed that one only prayed when it was needful. She sometimes got angry at the way people left their lives to prayer when they could simply do it by themselves.

Deborah was peeling yams on the veranda when Miriam got to the compound.

'I knew you didn't go to church,' Deborah said.

'I went to the train station.'

Deborah nodded.

'I have this feeling that Chigozie isn't dead. He may be lost, but I believe he will still be found.'

'I won't lie to you – I don't feel the same way,' Deborah said matter-of-factly.

'Why?'

'And the rumours are not helping.' Deborah clicked her tongue.

'What rumours again?'

'Two days ago, when I went to the stream to get water, some people said they'd heard the passengers were already killed. That the bandits had given an ultimatum to the government, which they failed to meet.'

'That can't be true.'

'Nobody knows the truth.'

'Don't you remember about the students who were said to be missing and even dead but suddenly reappeared?'

'They were only missing for five days.'

Miriam sucked her teeth. 'Chigozie means everything to me. If he is dead, I'm also dead.'

'I understand.'

'No, you don't. You don't have a kid.'

'Is that how you see it? What about the time I spent watching you when you were little?'

'This is different.'

'What's different here?'

'I lost Kingsley, and when Chigozie gets a dream of making our life better, something bad happens.'

Deborah embraced her tight. 'Okay, I believe he's alive.'

The following day was Saturday; Deborah cleaned the house before Miriam left her room.

'You are such a darling,' Miriam said when she came out.

'I felt hope in the air.'

'That's what I've been saying.'

Miriam went to look at the farm. The shrinking leaves had already straightened, facing the sky. The long wait for rain had been forgotten. The sky was bright, and the sunlight was tender. She walked around the farm, touching the stems of the corn plants and removing the weeds. Then, she threw the weeds away and washed her hands. She met Mr Okoro crying, close to her porch.

'What happened?' I said.

'The rumour was true. The bandits killed the passengers long ago because the government didn't meet their demands,' Mr Okoro said. 'I told you the truth was going to come hard on us.'

'Are they dead?'

'Their bodies are in coffins in the church.'

'You mean all of them?'

'What were you expecting?'

Deborah, who had been eavesdropping, was already out. 'People are running,' she said, pointing to men and women running past the compound.

'Where are they running to?' Miriam asked.

'To the church,' Mr Okoro said.

Miriam was surprised that she wasn't crying yet. As she walked hastily to the church, the only thing on her mind was whether Chigozie would be among them. She didn't want to think how his body would be or anything else. Except for his dreams – were they also dead? The loud screaming and yelling and cries could be heard a mile away from the church. Deborah got close to Miriam and held her hand. Tears were already crawling down her cheeks. On the steps of the church, policemen and women walked around, and medics bowed their heads in disgust. They entered the church at once, and the first open coffin was a young man with a bullet hole at the edge of his forehead. Miriam began to tremble. Deborah almost vomited, and Mr Okoro crouched and began to cry. A woman had fainted, and the medics were carrying her away. Her husband held his dry fingers on the belly of his daughter's corpse and said, 'She was three months pregnant.'

Almost at the corner where Kingsley had stood as a pulpit usher, Chigozie lay in a coffin: his eyes covered, a gentle smile at the edge of his lips, and a bullet hole in his chest. Miriam glared at the body in astonishment. Tears ran profusely down her cheek. Deborah had stopped and released her from her grip. Miriam touched the bullet holes. Chigozie's body still had a green shirt on. Something fell from the chest pocket. It was a small piece of paper. On it was written: *If thou hast run with footmen, and they wearied thee, then how canst thou contend with horses?* Deborah took the paper and read it. She stopped crying. They both glared at the corpse in puzzlement. What was it that made him keep the paper in his chest pocket? Perhaps he had been planning to take it with him to Jos, but the 'footmen' wearied him to death.

Eha-Amufu, a community that had become jubilant after the rain, now wailed in the misery of more hopeless history.

Victor Okechukwu

Victor Okechukwu is a writer based in Lagos, Nigeria. His writing takes a deep setting in arresting issues of mental health that have been overlooked in his country. He's an Associate Prose Editor at Zerotic Press and is reading mass communication at the University of Nigeria, Nsukka.

FIDELITY
Bhumika Anand

THE sun is bright outside the window, and the sky a gorgeous, pristine blue that I have come to call European blue in my mind. I will miss this sorely once I go back home to Bangalore. In August, Bangalore is grey and drizzly.

Berlin comes alive in the summer. And in Berlin, so do we – Nitesh and I, that is. The city just brings a different aspect to our personalities, to our relationship. He is happier, more playful. He reminds me of the young twenty-two-year-old I fell in love with. We're in Kreuzberg, and it buzzes with energy and colour. If Berlin is diverse, Kreuzberg is its most diverse neighbourhood.

We had breakfast at The Nest and now walk along Görlitzer Park. He rolls me a joint as we walk and lights it for me. I inhale and immediately feel knots I didn't know I had in my back untangling. Why have they not legalised weed in India yet? 'They should legalise weed in India,' I say.

'I don't see it happening in our life, Anjali. And now with Modi. Impossible. That's why I said move here. Live with me.'

Two years into our marriage, he got an onsite opportunity in Germany through Bosch, and I opted to stay back in India. We heard, 'What sort of a marriage is that?! Long-distance marriages don't work. You should follow him. Don't you worry about what he will get up to?'

The truth is, having visited Stuttgart for ten days that first winter, I knew I abhorred snow and winter.

Early on, we had decided on the sort of life we wanted to live. Coming from a city and having rich parents who were still independent made it easy. Privilege is a blessing. Every European winter, we'd visit the warm beaches in India – Goa, Gokarna, Cochin, Calicut, Mangalore, Pondicherry. Every European summer, we would tour the world, searching for experiences and making memories. In Berlin, we made the most memories. So, after the first year, we always spent the last ten days of our time together in Berlin. We made sure we didn't stray too far from Mitte or Kreuzberg. In a way, we were as much a part of the summer landscape in Berlin as the new graffiti each year. Every year, we strayed apart and drew together. Each vacation tested and tried us in different ways.

'Nits, please, not again. It's such a good day. Let's not ruin it by talking politics or my move. I don't want us to fight again. Besides, even you don't live in Berlin. And summer doesn't last all year.'

'True. Winter is coming.'

'Is coming,' we say in unison.

'God! I'll miss you, Anj,' he says, pulling me closer to him and twining our hands together. 'Will you miss me?'

'What?! Where's this coming from? Of course I will miss you too. You don't know how difficult it is for me back home without you.'

'I do know. But have you considered that it's not easy for me here, either?'

'I know, so you keep saying. I know. But you have these regulars – in the plural. And. Oh, look at those flowers! So beautiful. Do you know what they are called?' The flowers overflow from a large wooden barrel outside a storefront. They are arrestingly purple.

'Purple flowers?' he ventures.

'Very droll, Nits. How can you be the son of a horticulturist and not have any interest in plants? I will never understand this,' I say as I get my iPhone out to take pics of the flowers. I also quickly take a selfie, pulling Nits to me. He obliges with a goofy smile.

'Allo, beautiful lady. Alles klar?' A tall, muscular black man stumbles out of the store and stops theatrically in front of me.

Nits is relaxed as I tense up. 'Alles gut,' he replies cheerfully.

'Gut, gut, beautiful lady,' the man repeats. 'You from India? You tourist? You very beautiful.' He reaches out as if to touch me, and I step back warily.

'She is.' Nits is unruffled as he pulls me to him. He is proud I am being hit on. I feel uncomfortable and intimidated. The weed I have smoked adds to the paranoia. I rush into the park, hoping to lose the man. The park opens to a football field that's large and desolate. In the distance, I see benches and people. The man walks in with us, keeping pace while gazing comically at me as if he were really smitten. Nits just laughs. I refuse to respond. My fingers tighten over Nits'.

'Indian beauty very shy,' the man says, and just as we near other people, he settles himself on a park bench and whistles.

'Ah, that was unpleasant,' I say as soon as we are out of earshot.

'Why? He was appreciating how beautiful you are. They say black men tend to like curvy women – hence proved, I think.' Nits smirks. 'Did you ever meet that black man last year? He was seriously hot. Where was it? Frankfurt? This guy was very good-looking, too.'

'Really? I didn't notice. I was too busy being scared.' I shake my head. 'The Frankfurt Tinder guy? He was sweet and respectful. He cancelled on me. He had to rush back – Ethiopia, I think – before the peace deal. I wonder what happened to him. I hope he's ok.'

'He will be. Don't worry. But I do want to hear all about it when you shag a black man someday. It's the next best thing to being there.'

I have heard such things from Nits before. Today, it irks me. 'Fetishising much? I don't like that.' I pause, thoughtful. 'How come you don't tell me a lot about your lovers?'

'Eh? What is this now? Of course I tell you everything. You were the one who said you didn't want to know the details anymore. Remember? Last summer?'

'That's because you were showing me their profiles and pictures. I didn't want that.'

'Darling, are you jealous? That's a new thing.' He caresses my hand in reassurance.

'Of course I am jealous. These people get to see you and touch you whenever they want. I need to put in so much effort and spend so much money to be able to do that.'

'Anjali. You are the one insisting on living in India. There's not even much for you to do there anymore. And you hate your job.'

'I do. But it is my dad's business. I can't just give up on the running of it. And at least it is a job. What would I do here?' I am not sure why he keeps bringing up my move to Germany. 'Would you move back to India again?'

When we were still dating, in engineering college together, we decided we didn't believe in marriage. Nitesh wanted to be cool and free. He didn't think marriages were that. He wanted to live together. But the pressure from our families was too high. When we couldn't even find a decent place to rent as a live-in couple, Nits and I decided to give in and get married when we were both just twenty-five and fresh out of college. It was simply easier and more practical. So, we defined what this marriage would mean to us.

An open marriage was the compromise we both wanted. Even living in a city like Bangalore didn't allow us to try or nourish that aspect of our relationship. To be fair, as long as we were living together in India, we didn't feel the need to actively pursue a relationship outside. Besides, it was still early days. There was the excitement of sharing a life together. We were like children playing house. There were hardly any men I was attracted to. Nitesh might have wanted to, but not enough to really do anything about it.

The Bosch move necessitated us truly trying out what we spoke about. We were finally in an open marriage. It was a working arrangement, but we excelled at it.

'Darling, if I do come back, this lifestyle is over. You know that. We are well-off but not enough to sustain multiple international trips. Besides, how many people would understand our choices in India?'

'I am still being judged there, Nits. You are away from it all, so you don't know what it is to live the way I do. There are too many questions if I let anyone in, and it's isolating not to have people to hang out with. I mean, if it weren't for Shashank, I doubt this would work for us.'

'Shashank! There you go. This is why I am jealous of Shashank. I hate your arrangement with him. It's like he is your husband, and I am just a lover on the side. You give him far too much importance.'

'What?! You never said that before.' I stop walking. We are at an alcove made by a low-lying weeping willow on the banks of the canal. The small high I had begun to experience after the weed is evaporating very quickly. 'You know it's not true. And Shashank! I barely even like him. He's just good in bed. It's not like I can advertise that I am in an open marriage in India. Shashank is discreet, unemotional, and he understands our situation.'

Nits moves in on me, rubbing my arms. His fingers are warm against my skin. I am jolted by how much less familiar I am with his touch as the years go by. Is that why he is still so exciting to me? The past when we lived together seems like another lifetime ago. We simply never get a chance to get fully used to each other anymore. 'That's why I want you to move here. You will have more options. We will be together all the time.'

'You should have led with "We will be together all the time."' I look away, slightly hurt.

'Come now, Anjali, don't read between the lines. You know we both want this.' His voice is smooth and comforting. His hand moves to caress my cheek.

I feel my tension melt away. Can it be that simple? 'I do. But I really feel it's more frustrating for me than it is for you here. You have it mostly easy.'

'You keep saying that. But baby, that's only what you think. Have you thought of how lonely it might be for me here? You have family there, a support system. What do I have? Just that cold apartment. People barely even speak in English. If I want my lawfully wedded wife to move in with me, I get the whole "Be more understanding of my career and my needs," and if I do that, then you try and make it seem like I am completely happy with everything, and we know I am not.' I can sense the frustration from every pore of his body. It's like heat. Palpable. And very reassuring.

I massage his back. 'I know, babe. I know. I am sorry. This is hard. Look, we're on edge because I am leaving soon. It's almost our last week. You know that I am happy with you, our marriage, this arrangement even. I just hate the pressure and judgement I get when I go back. Your mom wants to know why we aren't having kids. So does my mother. No, don't get involved. That's not why I am saying this. I am handling it. It's just...' I shrug helplessly.

'You are right. Let's not argue about things we can't change.' He moves into my hug. I fit under his chin. He absently massages my back as he talks. 'I worry about you, you know. And family might be a support system, but all those judgements. The hypocrisy. And I really don't like what India is becoming. All that Hindutva now. I mean, it's all scary. That's why I want us to live here together.'

'Nits, please. It's not like there's no hypocrisy or judgement here. And in Stuttgart? In Germany, we are always outsiders. But it's not about the politics, is it?' I nuzzle his neck lightly. I can smell the light musk on his skin. 'It's about us. I don't think moving out of India is going to help anything. Do you want me to stop seeing Shashank?' I kiss him on his neck. Interesting. He hasn't worn the deo that he normally does. In fact, he's made no effort to look more appealing or sexy for his date. If it's the regular I think it is, he's probably going to break it off today. Things must be getting really sticky if he is going out when I am visiting. The rule is that I date when outside India, but he doesn't when I am visiting. I kiss his neck again and feel his smile.

'I don't know, that's up to you. We decided we won't interfere in each other's choices, remember?' His tone is wry. One kiss and his frustration has eased.

This is all I want. Would we still have this sort of marriage if things were different?

'Yes, only if safety and health are compromised,' I say, looking up at him. 'But misgivings should count for something, too, right?' It's my turn to caress his cheek.

'We've made these choices. We have to suck it if it gets tough. I know there's no decent polyamorous scene in Bangalore or even India. It's not safe. As you said, Shashank is a safe bet. And I definitely don't want you to risk anything. Let's not revisit these old arguments. It's a beautiful day, and we are together.' He kisses my hand.

'Except, my husband has a sex date in what? Twenty minutes?'

Nitesh clutches my hand tightly. 'It's not sex. Or at least I don't think. It's just. You know who it is. And it is what you think. I couldn't reschedule. It wouldn't have been fair or good. Please understand, love. You know I'd not do this when you are visiting otherwise.'

'I do. I am fine, really,' I say. I know what he means. We might not owe our lovers conventional relationships, but we have to follow certain codes, too. We can't just use people when we want them or only when it suits us. Courtesy demands that we cater to their desires too, at times. Courtesy also demands that we end things fairly and well if we feel it is getting too sticky or emotional. At least, this was the way Nits and I decided to operate early on so as not to invite bad karma.

He kisses me on my lips and then my cheeks. 'Will you be fine walking back? Stay here by the canal. Watch the world go by.'

'I am not going to wait for you here, Nits. I will head back to the house.'

'Ok. Wait. I still have time. Let's smoke another joint.'

I love that he doesn't want to leave me, that he's reluctant even to go on his date. It is indeed a good day. We stand by the canal, side by side, smoking, sharing that joint. The weed slows the world, and for a few minutes, it is like no one exists except for Nits and me. He stands behind me, pulling me up to his chest. We stand that way for a long time, watching the water ripple in the breeze. Then he turns me to face him. 'You know I love you, right?' he says, looking into my eyes. This is the same way he asked me out in college. There was no way I would have said no to him. He still looks at me the same way. How many women experience that? Nearly all the women I know worry that their husbands don't romance them. My friends distract themselves with work, children, fitness or even spirituality. My mother lives her life with a sullen complacence. My grandmother threw herself into managing children and a house where all the utensils always shone bright. I feel lucky in comparison.

I smile up at him. 'I know. Go now. Hope it's easy. Do you have the condoms?'

His face lightens in response. 'It won't come to that, but I do. You know I am always safe. Are you very high? Can you walk back ok?'

He is all concern as he looks me over to make sure I am not too high from the weed. 'I'm fine. Don't worry,' I say, patting his arm. He leans in for another quick kiss and deepens it. I taste the weed and the salt from his breakfast.

'We shouldn't,' I say, pulling back with reluctance. His eyes are clouded in abstract concentration. I know that look very well. It makes me happy. I kiss his nose. 'I don't think it's nice,' I say, rubbing his bottom lip. My thumb colours orange from my lipstick.

'Ok,' he agrees, caressing my arms. He kisses my cheek. 'I'll be back soon.'

I don't look at him as he leaves. Instead, I turn and walk back the way we came.

I enter Görlitzer Park again. I am not very high. I feel at ease and relaxed. I notice the same purple flowers growing by the park and quickly google them. Lobelias, I tell myself when I finally identify them. I am pleased with myself now, so I sit on a park bench in Görli. In the distance, I see children playing football. I light my Classic Milds and inhale. In another year, I will turn forty. I think then the expectations and questions about motherhood at least will stop. Once I turn forty, maybe things will change. Maybe even in India. Maybe Nits and I can live in India openly and happily. I laugh to myself at the impossibility of alternative choices ever being understood, forget accepted, in Indian society.

But I can handle this.

There are many lessons I have learnt in love over the years. The key one is the lesson on forgetting. I have learnt to live in the now. It means that I forget how my husband, the love of my life, might be in another lover's arms while I am walking in the park alone. It means that when he gets back, we will go on to have another easy, lazy day of vacation. It means that when he reaches out to me in the middle of the night, I will focus only on how much we want each other still and not think of how he might have touched another person this way. It's all knotty and strange. But Nits and I do have a very strong marriage, and we are still in love with each other. That's all I need. Live in the now, I tell myself. And who knows what the future will bring?

But it is easier said than done.

To shake off my mood, I google lobelias. I want to impress Nits with this information. In German, they are called Männertreu. It means 'faithful to men.' Or 'faithful men.'

'Nits, they are like you,' I will say. 'Faithful men.' It makes me smile. In my mind, I can see how he will laugh at me for this. My smile broadens.

BHUMIKA ANAND

Bhumika Anand is the Founder and Director of *Bangalore Writers Workshop* (BWW) the first-of-its-kind writing and storytelling school in Bangalore, India, established in 2011. Her work has been published in *Urban Confustions, The Affair, The Bombay Literary Magazine*, and *Out of Print* among others. She is an intermittent but uncomfortably intense blogger at Bhumika's Boudoir.

You can reach her on: www.bangalorewriters.com

Blog: https://bhumikasboudoir.wordpress.com

FRINGE CONTENDER
von reyes

B*REATHE, Alon. Breathe. Get your fucking head on straight.*

The ache in Alon's jaw blooms and spreads down the tense muscle of his neck into his shoulder. The swollen tissue on the inside of his cheek presses against his molars and pushes his left eye nearly shut. He spits the taste of iron and acid into the dust beneath his bare feet. The hydraulics of his arm are shattered, he can tell, the frayed shrapnel peeling away from the metallic skeleton beneath. The high-pitched wheeze of his knuckles lets him know he has two more punches left in this fist before it caves. Maybe three, tops. His handler, Dominic, lightning fast, solders the worst of it closed, the sparks flickering in the low light of the Underground. He squirts water into Alon's mouth with a reassuring slap on the back and steps out. Alon tries to ignore the searing pain the gesture shoots up his spine.

But he's come back from worse than this in the ring.

He rolls his shoulders and swallows down the rest of the blood on his tongue. He readies his stance, hands up near his face, light on the balls of his feet, agile but strong. His opponent stares him down across the ring, baring his bio-enhanced canines at him in a patronising grin. The deep purple of his mechanised eyes pierces through the hazy glow, and his sweat-slick black fringe sticks mucky to his forehead. His bare, dust-caked torso looks unmodified, but Alon had felt the iron defence of his rib cage rippling under his skin last round. Whoever is sponsoring this newcomer has a lot riding on their investment.

The ref droid steps into the centre of the ring, its arm raised in a fist. The anticipation ripples through the crowd, static floating off their tightly packed bodies into the dirt and up Alon's legs. He gulps a lungful of acrid air through his nose, letting it stream slowly out through pursed lips.

It's gonna take a lot more than fancy new toys to dethrone me.

The ref droid drops its fist and jumps back against the cage, blowing the whistle. An oppressive hush falls over the Underground, the black mass of the crowd undulating as they all lean forward in unison. Alon shifts his weight between the balls of his feet, digging his toes into the grime, becoming a part of it. He's on the defensive, watching for the nearly imperceptible tells of his opponent's next move.

Finally, the man strikes, taking one long stride, then careening the broad side of his foot toward Alon's nearly broken jaw. The crowd explodes; the adrenaline is contagious. Alon had watched him pop up on the back foot, knew he was going for a kick on the weak side. It's amateur, predictable. He parries with his organic hand, leaning away before the foot can make contact, and wraps his fingers around the delicate bones of his ankle. He brings his metal hand up in tandem and crunches the bones between his fingers, throwing his elbow up into the man's face and making contact with his nasal bridge. He makes no noise, no single utterance of the pain he must feel.

He pushes in and hooks both of his arms around Alon's mechanised bicep, trying to break out of his grip.

Alon drops the broken ankle and wraps his free arm around his waist, surging forward. He shifts the full weight of his body against the man's torso and feels him lock his legs behind his back. The muscle shifts under Alon's fingertips. He keeps pushing, dodging the man's gnashing teeth at his neck until he feels his grip waver on the metal. He slams his forehead against the man's, and the purple hue turns off into a dull grey for a split second. It's enough time to free his metal arm and extend the claw-like blades sheathed between his fingers. He rakes them down the column of the man's spine, metal catching on metal underneath tender flesh. The man's legs don't falter around his waist, and he leans up with an open mouth to rip the flesh at the nape of Alon's neck. He's uncoordinated from the head trauma and just misses Alon's carotid artery. Alon lifts up, pulling all the power he can into his core, and slams him down flat on his back. He repositions himself, pressing his knee to his throat and grabbing both of his wrists with his human hand. He deals two blows to his already injured nose with the blood-soaked knuckles of his iron-alloy fist.

His opponent's biceps go limp, the strength sucked out of him, and Alon digs his knee in deeper against his windpipe, pinning his arms above his head. He thrashes his knees against Alon's back with everything he has, every hit whiting out the corners of Alon's vision. He breathes through it, takes it the way he knows he can, *just a little more, a little longer.* He uses every bit of grit and muscle power left in his body to hold the pin. The man beneath him chokes out an attempt at breathing, his tongue lolling out onto his bottom lip between those too-sharp teeth. The purple of his irises flickers. The colour is beginning to rise up his neck and into his cheeks, his lips puffing up, and sweat and tears drip down into his ears. A dark purple bruise is forming across the bridge of his nose. In different circumstances, it wouldn't be a bad view.

These are Alon's only circumstances. And there are no rules down here except tap or die. Most people choose pride over life, and Alon wishes they wouldn't. Begs this one to make a different choice. He stares down into his eyes, pleading. The indignant determination he finds in his furrowed brows is nauseatingly familiar. Beautiful, in a way that only men like them could ever understand.

Free us both, pretty boy. Please.

The flickering is slowing in tandem with the man's consciousness. An empty kind of serenity begins to creep into his face. A wrist pulls from Alon's grip, and a warm palm taps softly against his hip. It lingers. It burns.

The ref yanks Alon up and off, throwing him back against the cage. Alon watches as the man sputters, then chokes on an attempt to put oxygen back in his chest. The ref kneels down to confirm the tap, and the man nods, trying to scramble onto his knees. He doubles over onto his forearms, the wet retch more heard than seen by Alon. The hologram above his head flashes bright blue, strobing the Underground with disorienting, cold light. This is the one moment every night when the tantalising cover of dust and glow lifts away, and the Underground is exposed for the filth that it is. It plays out in front of him in slow motion, like stills being captured on film between each surge of the LEDs. Drunken proletariat screeching, red-faced in the crowd, either in glee or dismay, depending on where they bet their credits. The cracks in the droid-ref's face, reminding him of its disposability. Blinding chromatic glare blazing off the tower above, where the sponsors watch their dogs fight without having to get their suits dirty. The melanated skin ripped open around the constellation of scars and freckles on the man's back as he lies in a heap in front of him, skin so similar to Alon's own. There's a flash of metal beneath the blood.

Alon's serial number bursts over and over on the screen as the announcer calling out his victory drowns out the dredge. Dominic hauls him over the cage with a face-splitting smile and tosses him into the awaiting crowd, starting the chant.

'KN-596! KN-596! King of the Underground!'

He lets himself be carried along, dripping blood and sweat off his form down into their hands and clothes. They soak it in, eager and feverish, and the euphoric high of victory washes out the ache in his spirit and battered body. He throws a fist up at the ivory tower above, where he knows the sponsors hide behind their walls of glass.

'You hear that? This is my house, fuckers!' he shouts to the faceless forms. It might be their world, but it's Alon's domain down here. The crowd carries him back into the ring, a spotlight following him all the way down. The ref rolls back into the centre and raises Alon's organic arm high in triumph. Dominic holds up his tablet so that Alon can watch the credits roll in in real time. A white-hot burn in his shoulder joint, where man meets machine, ignites in anticipation of his replacement arm. He hopes his sponsors will invest in some actual upgrades and modern technology, for once.

His opponent rises on wobbly legs, his amethyst eyes yet to return to a hundred percent. But still, he stands on the other side of the ref, daring to be dignified even in having claimed his own defeat. He'll be watched now – known as unwilling to die. A shameless weakling. But Alon stares at him, drinks him in without the filter of violence enacted upon them moments ago. His enhanced teeth make his jaw tip forward just the slightest bit, and his browline is strong and angular. The patch of hair in the middle of his chest is clumped together in blood and dirt, and Alon has a strong urge to wash him clean. His calf muscles slope down from behind his sharp knees to those narrow ankles, and Alon remembers how delicate the bones felt in his hands. How soft the skin was, pulled taut over tendons stretched to their capacity. He swallows, thick.

Alon envies him. He knows a day will come when he won't come out on top, and he wishes he had the conviction to choose to live when it does. The crackle of the droid's voicebox addressing him pulls him back to the moment.

'Congratulations KN-596. Please report to Med-Bay 1 for repair.' It rotates to the other man. 'JN-696, please report to Med-Bay 2 for repair.'

The man nods and exits the ring; another man just taller than his shoulder appears and wraps his arm around his waist. He flings his arm around the shorter man's neck and slumps into him, taking the assist as he limps into the cavernous abyss of the admin hallway ahead. They whisper to each other, and Alon's stomach turns at the gentleness. The intimacy. Dominic beckons him over, and the crowd starts to filter out. He hops back out of the ring and makes his way with Dominic down their own admin hall toward Med-Bay 1. His line of sight is limited, his left eye completely swollen shut now. Their steps echo off the steel walls of the corridor.

'You gotta stop waiting until the last round to remember your fundamentals. If you keep runnin' in hot like that as soon as the first whistle blows, you're gonna end up fertiliser.'

Dominic gives him this lecture every fight.

'Hasn't failed me yet.'

'Look, you came pretty close last night. You're not a god, Alon.'

The corner of Alon's mouth lifts in a smile more empty than it looks.

'Not yet. Maybe if moneybags gave me a real upgrade, I would be.'

Dominic rolls his eyes, exhaling through his teeth in exasperation. He doesn't respond to Alon's jab, having heard it one too many times. It's not fair anyway; Dominic's just a handler, only one step up from a dog-in-the-ring like him.

'Everyone knows your fighting style now. They're gonna start training 'em to target your lack of technique.' Dominic jabs a right hook into the air in front of him, shoving Alon with his elbow. 'You gotta counter.'

Alon waves his hand in the air dismissively, keeping up his end of the charade. On the surface, Dominic badgers him, and Alon ignores him, but he'll take him seriously at the gym on Monday. Both of them honour the message underneath. The black corridor opens into a glimmering white lobby, marble on the floor and harsh fluorescent lights overhead. Four sets of automatic glass doors line the walls, large silver numbers shining above each one. The reception desk sits ovular in the centre of the room, awaiting credentials. Dominic approaches with his data pad, and Alon hangs back a pace behind. His eyes follow a trail of burgundy droplets, like petals in the snow, until they disappear behind the glass of Med-Bay 2. He kneels down to run his finger through one of them, still warm, sticky and thick. He brings it to his nose, and the iron trace in his nostrils is just a touch off from human. Equal parts blood and mechanical oil. *What did they do to him?*

'Come on, Alon, or your shoulder is gonna atrophy.'

Alon follows Dominic into Med-Bay 1, rolling the fluid between his thumb and index finger until it dries. He lies down on the repair table and doesn't wince when the syringe digs into his neck, numbing him from the throat down. He opens his mouth obediently for Dominic, who jabs a smaller syringe into the meat of his cheek, numbing the left side of his face. A mask is affixed over his mouth, pumping gas into his brain until he's hazy. He doesn't mind this part, where he can feel his nerves dancing under his skin. He's weightless, like his soul is detached from his body, floating around the room. The damage scanner rolls down from the crown of his head to his toes, little beeps chirping on Dominic's data pad each time an imperfection is detected. He giggles, he can't help it, and he thinks he almost sees a smile on Dominic's lips through the blur.

An assist droid rolls in with new parts, and Dominic works quickly to replace the totalled hardware of his left arm. Alon wiggles phantom fingers as he watches Dominic attach the new prosthetic to the exposed metal base at his shoulder. Dominic scans it, quality-testing and making sure all the connecting points are online for Alon to access. The assist droid threads an IV into his vein on the opposite arm, lidoplasma rushing through his blood to heal the broken parts of him the mechanics can't reach. It makes his insides itch, and he wonders what it would feel like without the anaesthetics. He hears the glass doors slide open as the assist droid pulls the mask off to start repairing his face.

'An incredible fight tonight, KN-596. Kang Enterprises thanks you for your hard work, as always.'

His sponsor, Eric, makes himself known. His tinkling, serpentine voice lands like cotton in Alon's ears, muted and lilting through the chemicals in his brain. He hums around the metal instruments in his mouth.

'Now, I hear you're dissatisfied with your gear. Is that right?'

Alon's brows knit in frustration. He grunts in the affirmative. Eric knows he needs an upgrade. He asks Dominic to send the request after every fight. He can't imagine why he's suddenly decided to pay him a visit now. He wishes he was less vulnerable, flat and exposed on the operating table.

'You're a hero down here. Do you know why?'

It's rhetorical, Alon knows. His molars are being reset, and the soft tissue of the puncture wound at the base of his neck is being cauterised. The tone of Eric's voice makes Alon's palms tingle.

'It's *because* you aren't heavily modified. Mostly a man, with but one outdated mechanical limb. People still need to believe that humanity is stronger than technology. You're living proof of that. You don't need all the bells and whistles, like that yellow-bellied newbie we saw tonight. Johnson Industrials must have spent a fortune on him, and for what?'

What is humanity, if not cruelty for the sake of?

Eric clears the laughter from his throat, assuming a more professional tone.

'Rest assured, darling, I won't let you die out there. As soon as a challenger comes up that I think you can't handle, I'll get you an upgrade. You have my word. I look forward to that day, actually.'

He pats Alon softly on his bare abdomen, causing the muscles to flutter involuntarily. His hands are clammy and cold. He whispers something to Dominic, then whisks himself out the door, all billowing opulent fabrics and waifish silhouette. Alon would kill him if he could.

~

Fizzling orange street lights cast long shadows in the alleyway, and the cold, crisp air of the surface is burning Alon's lungs worse than his cigarette. He tugs his black leather glove further up his wrist to hide the new machinery and pulls his jacket closer to his chest. Dominic exits the Underground from the side door to his right, blinking as his vision adjusts. The bags under his eyes are as deep as the shadows.

'You headin' home?' Dominic asks, his voice weary.

'Nah, I'm still riding the high of it. You?'

'Can't get home fast enough,' he exhales, scrubbing a hand over his face. He pats Alon on his new shoulder. 'Don't damage the goods.'

Alon salutes him, the filter hanging off his lips, and watches him disappear into the night. He leans back against the concrete wall and closes his eyes, trying to decide where he'll end up tonight. He's bored of the bars and the brothels, but his tracker chip will only let him wander so far outside the city. Maybe he should just go home.

The door opens again, and he lazily casts his eyes over to look as the metal frame scrapes closed. Bright purple cuts through the orange. *Hey, pretty boy.*

'You put up a hell of a fight, JN-696,' he says, and he is sincere. He didn't mean for it to come out so condescending.

'That's not my name.' His voice is deep and rich, like the oil-slick blood he left on the med-bay lobby floors.

Alon takes a drag, puzzled. *No, of course it isn't.*

'I know that.' He kicks a rock with his boot and sizes him up. Ripped black jeans that hug his legs, big black boots that come up to his ankles, a soft blue, collared shirt hanging open on his shoulders with the sleeves rolled up. His torso beneath is bandaged from just below his navel to his pectorals. His dark hair has been washed clean.

'Aren't you cold?'

He shakes his head no and leans back against the wall next to Alon, hands stuffed in his pockets. Alon flicks open his cigarette box and offers him one, wordless. He puts a filter between his teeth and leans his head down, the unlit end hanging in Alon's eyes. The four pointed ends of his canines conjure images of torn flesh on his own neck, heat coiling in his stomach – so very different from the heat of the ring. He digs out his lighter and ignites the flame, watching the man's cupid's bow round out as he takes a drag. The bright, hot cherry blends in with the streetlamps, but the smoke smoulders like a secret hanging heavy in the air.

'So, what *is* your name?' he asks, voice softer than he anticipated.

The man looks up past the streetlight, searching for the stars hidden behind Fallen City smog.

'What'll you do with it if I tell you?'

The question drips with intent, but the connotation feels a little hazy. It lands more like an invitation than a threat in Alon's ears.

'Nothin' bad, promise.'

He smiles, finally, and Alon gets a good look at the mouthful of teeth behind his lips. The smoke drifts out of his nostrils.

'It's Hari. You?'

'Alon.'

Hari turns his eyes back to Alon's face, searching.

'Hope you're a man of your word, Alon, "King of the Underground."'

~

Hari's place is dingy and dark, a steel box on the twenty-fourth floor of a proletariat high-rise. But it's warm, washed in the smell of clean linen and instant coffee. They strip each other bare, skin glowing under the shattered moon. Alon slows the pace, just for a moment, to unravel the bandage on Hari's torso. He unwinds the layers, a little at a time, memorising the rise and fall of his chest under the touch. Once bare, Hari's fortified rib cage slides under the tips of his fingers as he digs them into his flesh, tugging him tight against his own. Hari pulls at the tresses on the back of Alon's head, tilting his face up to slide his tongue into his mouth. It's crushing, suffocating, and he imagines it's payback for the knee on Hari's neck a few hours ago.

Hari steps him backwards, daring him to trip over his own feet, until the back of his legs hit the bed. He sits, pulling Hari into his lap with demanding palms on his hips. Hari winds his legs around his waist, so much like he did in the ring, all thick muscle and determination. Sighs slip along their lips, melting into each other until the friction between them turns molten. Hari drags his canines across Alon's lip, wrenching a whine from his chest cavity. He drags the sharp ends down his neck, across his collarbones, down the taut plane of muscle on his torso, until he latches onto his hip. Alon bucks up into it, savouring the way they pierce through the skin.

Let this one heal on its own; let this one scar into a memory.

He digs his fists into Hari's shoulder, shifting his hips underneath him. Hari pulls off, those same lips cherry-red from Alon's blood, and drags his tongue hot against the marks left behind. He doesn't stop, wet, hot heat until Alon is swallowed whole. He looks up at Alon, all purple indignation. *Do it, I dare you. I want you to.*

So he does, burying himself to the pubic bone in Hari's throat. Hari hums around the mouthful, choking him down, hungry and eager. Alon isn't gentle, marvelling at the way artificial eyes can still produce tears. He could end it here, but he wants it to last. To hook his fingers into Hari and find the weak points he doesn't show anyone else. He yanks him off by the hair and leans down, lapping the blood and tears off of his face. Saliva drips down Hari's chin from his puffy lips, and Alon catches it with his thumb.

Hari rises, pink-dusted knees agitated from the floor, and pushes Alon up the bed until he's leaning against his pillows. He crawls back into his lap, and Alon pulls him back in for a kiss, running his tongue along the razor-edge of Hari's teeth. He still needs to know how sharp they are, even though they've been buried in his own flesh three times over. Hari's hips are moving faster now, chasing, so he pulls him off of his lap. Hari whines, bucking at the air in frustration.

'Turn over,' Alon whispers.

A rosy blush spreads up Hari's chest and neck, eyes shifting side-to-side, looking anywhere but at Alon. He turns over, leaning his chin against his forearms, his hips angled in the air. Alon knocks his knees apart further, tugging him closer until the backs of his thighs are pressed against Alon's collarbones. A vulnerable noise is trapped in Hari's throat, and Alon pulls it out into the open with gentle fingers. He hooks his mechanised arm around Hari's waist and hauls him up, pressing his back flat against his chest. He lines himself up and presses in, punching a trembling cry out of Hari's vocal cords.

'You can take it, right?'

Hari doesn't respond. Instead, he sinks down lower, tipping his head back against Alon's shoulder with a grind of his hips. Alon can imagine the burn Hari must feel. He cants his hips up at a steady pace, shivering as he feels Hari open up further for him. Hari reaches a hand back and grabs a fistful of Alon's hair, egging him on. *Make it hurt, so I know it's real.* Alon pulls him tighter against his chest, digging his claws into one side of Hari's ribs. It turns his moans from contented to wet and raw. Alon pumps him in time with his thrusts, the length of him hot and heavy in the palm of his organic hand. He watches over Hari's shoulder as a bead from the tip drips down over his knuckles and the muscles around him tighten. He speeds up, the knot in his stomach beginning to pull loose.

Hari presses the fingers of his free hand into the wounds where Alon's metal claws are embedded, spreading the blood over their knuckles. He interlaces their fingers, and the tableau of humanity and machine wrenches the last thread apart. It's too much, and Alon pulls him down hard, a throaty whine gurgling out with his release. Hari grinds down, following after with a soft *f-fuck* dripping off of his lips. He doesn't tap this time, though. He takes and takes until Alon has nothing left. Alon strokes him through it until his voice is hoarse.

~

Chilled, humid air snakes over Alon's sweat-damp limbs, cooling his skin to goosebumps. He exhales the cigarette toward the ceiling and watches as the smoke gets sucked out the cracked window above his head. The neon lights of the Fallen City refract off the glass and dance along the ceiling like fireflies. Hari smokes, too, lazily trailing his fingers across the bruise on Alon's hip bone. He has so many bruises, he's lost count and cause, but this one he'll remember.

'How'd you end up in the Underground?' Hari asks, just above a whisper.

'Lost my arm. Needed a new one.'

'Mm.'

More smoke, bodies shifting closer until their hips touch, long fingers stretching down and between thighs.

'You?'

'Was going blind, with a collapsed lung.'

'Mm. And you're still smoking?'

Hari giggles softly, barely more than an exhale of tickled breath.

'Can't damage titanium with nicotine.'

Alon laughs, too, at the honesty.

'Are yours paid off?' Hari asks, allowing the hope to creep into his voice.

Alon ashes his cigarette onto the steel floor, then turns to rest his cheek against the pillow to get a good look at Hari. He's staring at the ceiling, watching the smoke drift along the neon, trying to temper any emotions floating in his expression. The corner of his lip turns up as he interprets Alon's silence.

'They don't let you pay them off, do they?' There's still laughter bubbling up in the tone of his voice. It veers away from impish and edges toward hysteria. Alon grabs him by the back of his neck and pulls him to his chest, nuzzling his face into the crown of his head. He breathes in the sweat and shampoo, rubbing soothing circles between titanium shoulder blades. The tears pool in the cavern of his sternum.

~

Blood dribbles from the re-opened gash on Alon's neck, dribbles more from Hari's newly titanium-fitted bottom canines, staining the ridges of his lower lip crimson. The chrome finish flashes bright and blinding in the strobing static of the Underground. The weight in Alon's lap pinning him to the ring's dirt floor is heavy, like it had been in Hari's room. His cheek cracks under the force of Hari's titanium fist, but he can tell he isn't hitting with all he's got. Their legs tangle together like lovers under the sheets. He hears the crowd chanting his serial number, egging him on, begging him to get up. To fight back. *Champion of humanity, rise to your feet. Rise, so that we may hope to do the same.*

He won't oblige them, lying there as Hari tears him apart at the seams. Again. In a new way. The pain has long faded to a numbness as his resolve to win trickles away – killer instinct replaced with something much more salient and pure. The bright purple haze of Hari's gaze bears down on him, a new kind of agony quaking in his pupils. He hits Alon again, breaking his jaw properly this time. His molars rattle loose in his gums. Alon lets his hands lay limp at his sides – he wants to give this to Hari. He's been fighting for sponsors long enough.

Free us both, pretty boy.

Hari mirrors his own pleading expression from their last fight back down at him, begging desperately to be spared. His waterlines burn bright, tears streaking clear lines through the grime on his cheeks. One drips onto Alon's neck. A new fighter, soft-hearted, touch-starved – and utterly unwilling to be a sacrifice, Alon is abruptly reminded as his own vision turns watery. Hari's blood-slick fingers against his hip, in and out of the ring, are a sense memory tattooed under his skin. If Alon could learn to love him one day, the end might look different. It's ironic, now, to have a choice. He lifts one gnarled hand off the dirt floor, his palm hovering in the air next to Hari's ribs.

VON REYES

Von is an emergent author that uplifts the intersections of queer/trans masculinity and Asian diasporic identity through poetry and speculative fiction. He focuses on themes of surrealism, queer sexuality, existentialism, and optimistic nihilism. He hopes to tell stories that don't shy away from the horrors, but allows us to find the light within them. You can find more of his work in Same Faces Collective, the Good Men Project, and at vonreyes.carrd.co.

OLD TRICKS
Eve Morton

I was sitting in my booth at Haven, watching through the bar's glass windows as new ships landed on the dock from the deep dark ocean of space, reliving my own glory days behind a vessel when the dog came in.

'Damn dog,' I said under my breath. Then, hurriedly, almost like a cough, I corrected myself. 'Caninite.'

'That's better.' Angie passed me another drink and gave me a warm nod as I met her translucent eyes. Endless exchanges passed between us in that moment, all of which ended with a lesson in language. Yes, yes, I *knew* that the humanoid figure who walked in on two legs but had thick patches of fur around his face and hands, and who knows elsewhere, was a Caninite. That was the accepted species name; that was what my translator box would have told me, but I'd swapped it for my old wooden leg because I wanted to be a pirate. Or, rather, a privateer. Buccaneer. *Pirate*, Angie would always remind me, *is a slur*. Just like 'dog' was for the Caninites. Using the proper terms – for aliens, space creatures, and anthro-animals or genetically modded ones alike – was just good form. And if I didn't use the right words for my own civilising sake, then Angie, the interspecies bartender, wouldn't serve me anymore.

'You may be old world,' she'd said the first time I came into Haven and took the spot she'd eventually always clear as mine. 'But this is the new world. This is a place that has no limits, no borders or boundaries, and so we need to call one another by our proper names. It's the only damn thing we can agree on now.'

'I don't even think we can agree on that sometimes,' I said.

'Well, buckaroo, we're just going to have to agree to disagree.'

'Buck,' I said. 'My name is Buck.'

She grinned. *Of course it is,* her sharp teeth seemed to say. 'Sure thing, Buck.'

I really liked Angie. Still liked her four years later, even as my old wooden leg was creaking and reminding me I needed a change of scenery. Angie was a blue-skinned girl, the kind from Delta 7, and her species was often thought to be lawless. *Those see-through eyes can see through souls, curse you in place or otherwise steal what's not welded down.* She'd opened Haven to be the bar at the so-called end of the world, where people went when they were at the bottom of their luck, because she'd needed that place. And so, she paid attention to how people wanted to be known rather than how they were labelled or hailed. I liked her for that, among other things. I liked Haven. I didn't even mind that there were more than a handful of crooks and thieves and criminals who came here off the ships outside because they, too, wanted solace and to be known by the right name.

I fit in amongst them, after all.

'Buck?' Angie asked. She tapped her long, artificial fingernails on the metal table. I stopped bouncing between memories and scratched my wooden leg where the flesh met the smooth surface. Angie had been talking at me for some time, and I'd been elsewhere. She snapped a finger, almost broke an artificial nail, and sighed. 'Anything else? Or are you still drinking for one?'

I looked around, noticed the prison ship with a tickle against my skin but nodded. 'Still solo. Private eye. Private—'

She cut me off by placing a glass of water down on the table. The universal hangover cure, which meant she was priming me to leave. *You've had enough nostalgia for the night and enough fucking up of the other servers' pronouns. It may be time to go, big man.*

But I was not yet – not ever – completely done with this place.

Once Angie was gone, I continued to watch as more ships docked. The prison vessel, where the Caninite had disembarked, had already begun backing up for departure. Part of its front was dented, in need of repair. I didn't think it would last another mission, which was good, all things considered. There were hardly any prisons anymore. The rest of the ships were tourist in nature, stopping on this terra-formed planet in order to take a rest and refuel – but strongly encouraging their inhabitants not to get out and truly explore. Other ships, clad in silver that glimmered in the starlight, were pleasure ships or cruises from private investors. I didn't like them; they often came to me, sat down at my booth without asking and wanted to use my skills for some interspecies spy game or ridiculous custody battle. I often made them buy me a drink, entertain me with stories and then declined their offer. Angie didn't want her bar to turn into a den of iniquity, I often told them when they protested. More than it already was, anyway.

For a moment, when I grasped the water glass and took a drink, I was convinced I'd seen into a scrying glass. I saw myself – me, younger me – before all that nastiness happened on Earth. My leg was there too. By the time I finished the water, though, and the world had righted itself again, and I wasn't looking at me thirty years ago, with a red beard and two legs I could stand on proudly, I was looking at the damn dog again.

Excuse me. Caninite. He was inside Haven now. A prison-issued uniform covered his body, and the coat he wore was the kind they gave you upon release. Cold, flimsy, dark. The hood covered his ears and most of his furry head, but you couldn't hide that same loping gait that I had. This dogman had a limp; this dogman from jail needed a cane but didn't have one, and so there was a part of me that was struck dumb. The prisoner, the dogman – was he here to find a cane? Was he here for lamentations? Did he lose his leg in jail, before jail, and if he had modified his body from man to dog, why not also fix the limp?

The questions bothered me, so I drank again. All my detecting skills came back as if I was back on Earth again. As if my name was Marcus again. I shuddered, tried to gather what few items I had with me at the bar, and rose to leave my booth – but my leg buckled. I sat down. And when I realised he had already made it to the other side of the bar, where my blue girl Angie was, I knew he hadn't just come for a rest. He'd come looking for me.

And, like before, I accepted my fate. My wooden leg creaked as I sat down in the booth again, and the dogman practically galloped over to me.

'Marcus?' the Caninite said. 'Or should I call you Buck—'

'Ignore Angie,' I said, then shook my head. 'You can call me whatever you want. But take a seat.' When I gestured to the booth, I fought the urge to also say 'good boy.' The Caninite sat down and placed both of his hands on the table, flat. *Prison move.* His knuckles were hairy with thick, matted fur, but only to the knuckles, like a bad grafting job. He waited, poised, like a dog seeking out command.

I sighed, itched my leg, and then asked, 'And you are…?'

'Jack.'

'Jack—?'

'Dogs don't have surnames,' he said simply.

'And neither do prisoners.'

'Right. Well.' Jack looked around the bar, his gaze darting as he did. His nose heightened in the air, sensing around him. I tried to sense what he did – but all I got was BO and cigarettes from Earth. Maybe something chemical, the thing that Angie used to clean the bar. Nothing of note, nothing that made me feel calm – which was the exact thing this guy did. He sniffed the air, then sighed. As if this was home. As if this was—

'I missed people,' he said. 'Not just talking to them, but being around them. Prison is weird.'

'I think that's the point.'

'No, the point is recovery, attrition—'

As the dog went on, telling me all the rights and revisions that prisons now had, I could barely keep a straight face. He was right – I knew he was right, advocated for these rights when I'd had a leg to stand on, literally and figuratively – but it was funny. How could it not be? The whole scene reminded me of an old joke someone had once told me about a doggie outlaw coming into a Wild West sheriff's office and demanding, 'I'm looking for the man who shot my paw.' Stupid. Dumb. But jokes like that got me through the long nights in the deep sea of space and at a desk on Earth.

'Are you going to ask me something?' Jack said rather plainly. His hands were turned up now, as if he was someone awaiting a treat. 'Like why I'm here?'

'I figure you'll tell me in time. You're probably sick of people telling you what to do, considering the clothing. Not the species,' I added. 'Don't think I'm making fun of the Caninites, now, or Angie won't serve me.'

Jack chuckled lightly. When Angie came moments later to check on us, she gave him a drink of water and a bowl as well. Jack didn't seem offended but relieved; he took the bowl, poured the water into it, and lapped it up. She narrowed her eyes at me, seeming to say *behave* with a tilt of her head. I bit my tongue to keep from asking either one of them if they'd hit me with a newspaper if I did the wrong thing.

When the dogman finished his drink, Angie took the bowl, and he cleaned up the spills all by himself.

'Good boy,' I said, then bit my tongue. 'I know you just got out of prison,' I added hastily, 'but you don't need to call me Marcus. Appreciate it, but here, I'm really Buck.'

'Buck Knife.'

'Yes. So you do know?'

'Former pirate, now a fence. It's hard not to know.' For the first time, his eyes glimmered. When he didn't have a bowl in front of him and he was sitting down, most of the mods disappeared. He was just a man, staring at me with intense eyes.

'Pirate's a slur,' I said meekly. 'But what do you want?'

Jack sighed as if he'd wanted the exchange to go on for longer. From inside his outfit, he took out a set of keys, rusted as if they had been caught in a drainpipe for the last five years. He placed them on the centre of the table with gravity and aplomb befitting the fifteenth wonder of the world.

'I can't give you anything for that.'

'It's only half of what I need.' Jack pawed at the keys, more like a cat than a dog. He ran his hand, which had small fingers but was not quite a paw, around the edges of the most jagged-looking key, one that seemed as if it had stepped out of a novel from another time. I was disappointed I could no longer use my joke. His hands were more hand-like, and not paws. *Damn.*

'I would assume the other half of this,' I said, 'is a lock?'

'Yes. It opens the chest where I stashed my last prize.'

'Oh?'

'It's not a doggie treat.'

'Never said it was.'

'Good.' Now, Jack's eyes dilated. They didn't look like a dog's, but the man he was before all of this. Blue and iridescent. Stunning. 'This is one of the many reasons I'm coming off that nightmare prison vessel. You know, aside from The Council not liking dogs at all anymore.'

'Man's best friend turned to our worst enemy.'

'And only animals belong in cages. Yes, yes, I've heard it all. And I've had a long time to think about certain life choices while I waited to get these keys again.'

'And the treasure,' I said. 'Don't forget that. I love a good treasure story.'

'I bet you do. But it's rather boring.'

'Let me be the judge.'

Jack nodded, took a sip of the water and told me a rather long and not so much boring story as it was commonplace. He and three other men – men, not Caninites – robbed a wealthy patron one of the men did taxes for. This was the only funny part of the story: one of the robbers was a full-on accountant, complete with thick glasses, who was so determined to break out of the boring stereotype that he fantasised about being a cat burglar.

'He said "cat burglar?"' I asked, and Jack nodded with a smile, understanding my delight.

'Great. This is great,' I said. I leaned back in my chair and crossed my legs, revealing the wood, but I didn't care. 'Just perfect. Did you fight like cats and dogs? Oh my. Go on.'

Jack's grin was wide, though the story itself was far from happy. The four of them had hatched a plan. They'd rob the patron. Not of everything – they didn't want to get greedy – but a bunch of cash and equipment, stuff that was easy to fence and resell or use for other purchases.

'But this man had a diamond,' Jack said. 'A huge thing. We didn't know about it until we got into his basement, and well, we had to take it. Just too tempting.'

'I understand,' I said and rubbed the leg I'd lost over something quite similar.

'The thing was,' Jack went on, 'the diamond was very valuable – but also unique. We couldn't do anything with it. So we buried it and promised to get it later.'

'And now,' I said, seeing where the story was going, 'you're free after they ratted on you, and you want to get what's yours?'

Jack nodded his head. 'I don't like rats.'

'Of course not,' I said, still delighted. I leaned forward now, creaking my leg and revealing some of my scar tissue in the new light of the bar, but it didn't matter. This story was way too good. 'What happened?'

'It's boring, I told you: we were all caught because we hadn't done this before. We made way too many mistakes. Didn't even take long. Maybe six weeks? Maybe seven? Either way, while they were sent to rehab, I was sent to jail and then to the jail colony on Delta 99 when prisons were eradicated on Earth.'

'Rehab?'

'Theft is a disease,' he said, citing the charter law. 'And if something is a disease, it means you can be cured into ease.'

I'd heard that but didn't care for the slogan or for engagement. I rubbed my knee where the wood met flesh. 'So, how long did you serve?'

'Ten years,' he said, then leaned forward with a smile. 'Or seventy in dog years.'

I chuckled and lifted my glass to him. He clinked with his bowl.

I decided right then that I'd help him, no matter what. The story was too good to pass up, and I'd been living too much of my life lately looking out of Haven's window and getting lessons in language.

I wanted to tell my own story again.

'So what happened?' I prompted. 'You have the keys, you're out of prison, so are you asking me to help find the diamond I'm assuming one of your other men now has in his safe? It's been a while since I've done a heist, but—'

'No, actually. I know where the diamond is. It's under your house.'

'What?'

'The diamond. Where we buried it,' Jack reiterated. 'It was once a vacant lot. I dug the hole, of course. I selected it because I knew it was perfect. Right smells, good dirt texture, you know, all those lovely things that make me growl in a good way. So I dug, they plopped it in, I put the dirt back on, and we sealed it up tight. We left – and then we were caught, and everyone else either forgot about it or, well, they died.'

'They're dead?'

'Yeah. They all had good lives. No more risky business after they got out of rehab. Even Pete – the accountant – seemed to give up his ambition to be a burglar. Rehab is far better than the traditional prisons, but it is still a cage. And one cage is enough to make you think twice about crime.'

I nodded as I tapped my wooden leg again. A different kind of cage, but the main reason I was no longer a privateer on the space seas or a detective back in the old world. Contrary to popular beliefs about both power-hungry professions, most weapons actually cause more harm than anything else, and those wooden legs slow you down and make you truly ineffective on board. The plastic and metal and fancy robot legs were too expensive to shell out for given I never wanted them in the first place. And when I realised I could also junk the translator box the force gave me and retire with something that slowed me down in the best way possible, I took the buyout.

I retired.

Pawned my gun and lived off the proceeds until I got to Haven.

Became a fence.

A boring story. So much more boring than this shaggy dog's shaggy dog tale. After an awkward pause, during which he scratched his floppy brown ear, and I scratched my leg, I asked, 'So how did they die?'

'Slowly. One had an accident, Pete got shot in the crossfire of another crime – wrong place, wrong time – and the other guy was infected with a poisonous agent that shouldn't have been lethal. All easy to write off, but it seemed targeted. Like... someone coming back for revenge.'

'Looking for the man who shot his paw,' I said, but Jack didn't laugh. His dark eyes, so human-like yet shaped and coloured far more like a wolf's, only stared at me as he considered this possibility.

'Maybe it's a relative of the murdered man. Or maybe it's someone they bragged to while in rehab. I don't know who's marking them off. But this person or people or something else altogether never knew where the keys were because they were still in the same drainpipe we hid them in.' Jack held up the rusty keys for proof. 'But I need to get to that diamond. I need to get under your house. Because if I don't, the other party might, and then, we're both in danger.'

'Why not guard me instead?' I asked, trying to laugh off fear. 'Why not just bark away crime?'

Jack didn't say anything.

Neither did Angie, who I spotted across the bar greeting new people. Blue people like her, small and squat aliens from one of Jupiter's moons, and then humans. Earth humans, tourists. But also Earth people who weren't dressed like tourists in the neon Hawaiian shirts they offered at the station or carrying luggage bags with anti-gravity keychains.

There were too many people in Haven. Too many people seeking solace. And that meant I had to go very, very soon.

I looked at Jack again. Dogman. Caninite. Good boy? I shook my head. No one here was a good boy or girl or anything. No one here was good. But we could *do* good, especially if we did it for the right reasons.

And Jack seemed like a good reason. He seemed genuine, not like this was a ploy to get into an old pirate's house for some booty. His hands remained palm down on the table, supplicant, pliable and utterly vulnerable. He had far more to lose than me. This was not remotely what I'd thought would happen to me when I sat at Haven for the night, but it was better than window-watching, that was for damn sure.

I took a long swallow of my drink and placed the empty glass on the table. 'All right, Jackie boy. Let's see what we can dig up.'

~

Not surprisingly, Jack was a good digger.

Once we were in my house, I offered him a drink like you are supposed to when welcoming house guests, but he declined. I was about to offer a bowl, like Angie had, but Jack went right for my basement. The door was locked, but it didn't matter. He pressed his nose against the floor, close to the crack, and then along one side of the wall where the outlets for old electronics had once been. He sniffed and then seemed to cease breathing. His back stiffened, and for a second, I was drawn to his behind. Like, literal behind.

'My tail doesn't wag,' he said suddenly. 'It's a thing.'

'Oh.'

'It's fine,' he said and turned around from the door. Where he'd once been animalistic in his search, he was now refined, utterly composed. The only thing that remained from his previous searches was a small red blotch where he'd hit a nail. 'Just the way things work sometimes. We can grow hair, some of us have an extra-strong sense of smell, but the tail? Eh. Just sort of stays there.'

I couldn't help but look at his behind again. A bump was there. A bump that was barely visible through the loose prison outfit but one that… felt strange. Odd. That queer feeling of something like lust stirred in me. I blanched. I was used to liking men – that was no shock to me – but a dogman? No. That was not right at all. I was pretty sure if I bothered to look it up in my old detective handbook, I could arrest myself.

But then again, I had done worse things and not gotten arrested. And far less and only got a wooden leg.

'It doesn't matter,' Jack said. 'It's not in your basement. It's— Hmm. Oh.'

Jack leapt from the basement to the living room. He got on all fours, pressing his nose against the carpet until he reached a corner. Then, with his hands, he felt the wall, followed a seam until he sniffed once more. I watched, utterly bewitched, as he circled one area in the corner three times before he nodded.

'Here,' he said. 'We're going to have to dig here.'

'Um.'

'I can start,' he said, now getting down on all fours. 'You'll be surprised how strong I am.'

'Um. But. My floor. Uhhhh.'

'I thought of that. When I realised the lot was now a housing development, I made a stop before I came here.' Though Jack had nothing with him but the prison-issue clothing, it didn't seem to matter. In fact, that seemed to be part of his plan. 'I used to work in prison laundry. And when you clean a lot of sheets for animals, you use a lot of strong chemicals. And they aren't toxic to humans or animals, so they don't monitor them as much as they should.'

With a grin, Jack lifted a small bottle of soap from his black hoodie. It seemed more like baby shampoo than anything else, but as he cracked the top and dropped half of the bottle on my floor, the hissing sound was extreme.

'I will fix this afterwards,' Jack added. 'Don't worry. I have the solutions, too.'

But I was just amazed. I held a handkerchief over my mouth to stifle the smell, which was a mix of sand, patchouli and something like asphalt. As if they had paved Woodstock for a highway, I wanted to say aloud, but I wasn't sure if Jack would get it. He seemed to be my age, seemed to be from Earth, and maybe we could have even been neighbours back in the day. But at some point, we had both taken very different paths.

Once the floor was eaten away, and I'd opened a window or two to get the fumes out of the house, Jack was ready to dig. I offered shovels and even a trowel for my underdeveloped garden outside, but he shook off the offers.

'Prefer the hand-held touch,' he said and then dove into the dirt.

He dug quickly until he hit clay. Then he shifted around to another side to give his back a rest and went slower. He picked up the piles of clay and moulded them so the other dirt would not sink back in. His digging was clean, practised and – dare I say – almost fated. This man was meant to be a dog. He'd been born a human, so he would always be conscious that he would never truly be a dog, but he could be a Caninite. Not the ideal, but the closest thing to it.

I rubbed my leg, some of the pain of my injury coming back. I was relieved that I didn't have to offer any assistance because, by the time I stopped feeling a swell of pain in my joints, Jack was pretty much done. A clank sounded from underneath his hands. He'd hit the metal tin they'd buried the diamond in, and now he let out an excited yip.

'I may need your hands here,' Jack added once his celebrations were over. 'I can lift it out, but you'll have to tug it onto the floor.'

'Should have been helping all along,' I said and tottered over to the rather large hole in my floor and the piles of dirt around it. Jack's nose and forehead were streaked with dirt, marking the whiter and reddish fur with brown and mud. I couldn't help but survey most of his body as he worked, marvelling at the new ways genetically modified creatures could be made. And then, after being so enchanted with it all, I saw his tail.

A lump. Nothing much at all. It was the only thing that didn't seem so utterly perfect on him, the only thing out of place. A tail for a dog that didn't wag? Now, was that really a dog at all…? I scratched my leg and let it go.

'On three, okay?' Jack said and gestured to the metal tin.

'On three,' I confirmed. Hunching over was difficult, but together, we heaved up the metal box. I grabbed a handle on one side and pulled. My back ached. My lungs smarted. I shook my head and let out a mumbled apology as I dropped it.

'It's okay,' Jack said, though the corner had clocked him on the forehead. He touched his skin, came back with blood.

'Shoot,' I said again. 'I'm sorry. I can do this. Gimme another shot.'

'On three,' Jack said again, though his voice was not steady. 'One, two—'

I mustered all of my strength, but it did not seem to help. I couldn't believe this was so hard. Had I truly grown soft in Haven's low light, drinking and thinking my time away? Was this my leg? Was this old age? I made a vow to myself not to be so passive once this night was over. Not be so accepting. Where was my pirate spirit? It had gone to hide, it seemed, like so many other men had gone to hide when the Wild West of space had been tamed through law, order and other names.

'Almost there,' Jack said, encouraging me. 'Come on, Marcus.'

I struggled. I keened. I almost dropped it again.

'Buck Knife!' Jack cried out. 'Come on, Buck!'

My skin turned hot with joy at the sound of my old name.

'Come on, pirate!' he shouted now, seeing me finally react. 'Give it the old heave-ho!'

'Heave-ho!' I echoed.

And I pulled the crate all the way up and onto my floor. I dropped it the moment it was securely out of the hole and collapsed on the floor, out of breath. My chest hurt. My knees hurt. My cheeks hurt from smiling.

But I was smiling.

And so was Jack. Because when I dropped it, I'd also cracked it. Now the diamond was exposed.

It glowed bigger and brighter than I'd anticipated. Several facets shone, cascading light all over my living room. My black and worn-down furniture now came alive with light; it was like a disco ball in the middle of my living room, and there was only so much I could do before wanting to dance and sing.

Even Jack shuffled from side to side. He looked at the diamond, the one that had caused him so much heartache, like it was a big, juicy bone.

'I can't believe it,' he said. 'I made it. I got it. I'm the last one standing and—'

A heavy knock sounded on my door. The kind of knock, at the sort of hour of the day, that one could not ignore. My entire body smarted and felt caked with dirt. The small distance from our dig spot to the front door was monumental.

Jack looked at me with a frightened expression. 'It's them.'

'Who?'

'Them.' His eyes widened, and the animal parts glowed with fear. 'The ones who got my friends. The ones who didn't bother to find me but know how to track down dogs. They shoot dogs. Fuck. I—'

'Calm down.' I touched Jack's shoulder. It was warmer than I expected, and when Jack turned to me, towards me, almost curling in like an animal, I realised we were both terrified. Our bodies had been taken over with goosebumps and flushed skin; fear and dread welled in my stomach, making me want to throw up – and making Jack bark.

'Sorry.' He clapped a hand over his mouth. He barked again, flushed red through his reddish fur once again. 'It's a side effect. I can't stop—'

Another bark.

Another knock at the door.

'Fuck,' I said. I let out another strand of curses, ones I hadn't used since I was a pirate. And it felt so, so good. For the first time, something profound happened between the two of us: we spoke without words. We communicated without language. And suddenly, I knew we were going to be okay.

'We have to hide this,' I said, referring to the diamond. Another knock sounded, along with my real last name, but I ignored it. 'Now.'

'I'm not putting it back into the hole I just dug.'

'Well then, at least be a good boy and get my slippers or something.'

'What?' Jack's gaze narrowed, annoyed at my insinuation. When I touched his shoulder again, he turned towards me but also seemed annoyed by it. 'You can't just make me into your bitch, you know—'

'*Pretend*,' I said. 'Just pretend to be my dog. A good *boy*. A pet.'

Jack huffed, but when I continued to touch his shoulder, he curled further into me. He hugged me, I hugged him, and for a moment, it was just us. We were dirty, filthy, and things were beyond bizarre –

but I sort of loved this. It was nice. Touch. Comfort. I could feel how rickety I'd become on my wooden leg and from my sedentary life at Haven and at home. This was the most fun I'd had in a long time, and it was all about to come crashing down.

Another knock.

'I'll be right there,' I said and then coughed. 'I'm a very old man.'

The knocking stopped. I let out a low breath, one that also seemed to calm Jack. 'I may have been Buck Knife once, but no party ever officially caught me,' I told him in a low whisper. 'All statutes of limitations have passed. As far as the law is concerned, as far as whoever is on the other side of that door is concerned, we are both good men and dogs who have served their time. Never mind the diamond in my basement.'

Jack laughed derisively, but it sounded more like a whimper. 'You think it's the law on that side of the door. It's not. It's them.'

'The people who got your friends?' When Jack said nothing, I nodded. It was true – I did think it was the police. It would make the most sense to see the long arm of space justice at my door when everyone had seen me go home with a dog. 'But you're forgetting that I also used to be the law. I know they ain't good.'

Jack lifted a brow. He opened his mouth to say something, but the voices on the other side of the door cut him off. 'Marcus—'

'I am a crippled man!' I shouted. 'And I need to make sure my dog has some water before I see to your yapping. I know it's important. But respect your elders.'

Silence. It was heavy and profound, so much so that both Jack's and my gaze went to the front door. The light from outside flickered as multiple sets of feet became visible in the shadows. My heart leapt into my throat. I was barely able to stand on two legs, what if—

'What if they shoot me?' Jack asked. 'They shoot dogs—'

'If they wanted you dead, you'd be dead already,' I said in a whisper. I tapped Jack on the back, miming that he needed to get on all fours. 'Same with me. If they wanted us dead, they would have us dead already. Real criminals don't knock. That's how I know it's the law. They knock. Because they want us to run so they can catch us. But if we answer the door and be an old man and his old dog, maybe it's just a new trick we're playing.'

After a moment of tense consideration, Jack nodded. I tapped him again when he didn't get to the floor. He hesitated. Grumbled and groaned.

But he got on all fours.

And the feet behind the door also stopped flickering. They stood and waited to be greeted. I gestured to the couch in my living room, where Jack could curl up. 'But in front of the couch. Not on it. Good boys know they're not supposed to get on the couch.'

'Ugh, fine,' he said, though I heard the mirth in his voice.

'And you know that dogs don't wear clothing.'

'Oh, fuck you, man,' he said, with definite humour this time.

'That's a funny-sounding bark.'

Jack barked for real this time. 'See? I can play along. But you need to get the door, old man. And give me some privacy here.'

I turned my back, making my way towards the front door as Jack was still chuckling. His laughter then softened into small yips. Before I opened the door, I grabbed the cane the police force gave me as a going-away present. It felt like betrayal in my hands then, but now, as I leaned on it, I could lean into the old cripple role I'd decided to play. Holding the cane always eased my fear; it also absorbed all the sweat that had started to collect. This was serious. A crime.

This was an adventure again.

'Hello?' I answered the door. I leaned out and squinted against my own front porch light. 'How can I help you tonight?'

'Hello, Mr Brown. Marcus Brown.' A man in an international space uniform looked down at his device as if to verify my ID on the screen. Another man stood next to him, in a green uniform with a strange logo in the corner. Maybe a boat? Or an ark? It had only recently been created when I left the force. 'Marcus Brown who owns the lease for this residence?'

'That's me, yes. I'm afraid I have no money to give the alien children or to save the whales from—'

'No, we're not soliciting.'

'Then what can I help you with?'

'We've had reports that a former criminal named Jack Douglass has been spotted in the area. He was supposed to be serving a sentence on Delta 99 but escaped before serving his full sentence.'

'We still keep people in prisons?!' I asked, acting horrified. Very little acting needed, even at the possible deception on Jack's part – breaking out of prison was not truly a crime-crime in my book. 'That's terrible. I thought we outlawed those back in—'

'He's a genetically modified animal,' the man in green said. 'I'm from Ark Station, the prison where we keep beasts like him. Animals belong in cages, sir, especially animals with the reasoning ability to perform heists and follow through with murder.' The man waited, trying to bait me, but I pretended to lean closer so I could hear better. The man went on, now an octave louder, 'Jack Douglass had been sent to Delta 99 from an Earth prison to complete his sentence. But when we went to deliver the laundry a few days ago, we found his tracker device, his paw prints—'

'Wouldn't he have hands?'

'No, paws,' the man in green continued. 'We found evidence of his escape and have been tracking him since. We now believe he has come to this planet to seek a safe haven.'

'Oh, that's a good bar. Angie's very nice. Have you—'

'We have gone to the bar, and most patrons told us to come here.' The man in green raised a brow. 'Any particular reason why we should come here?'

'I'm an old man, old pirate and cop, so I may have some information on why we shouldn't use prisons anymore.'

'That's not why we're here. You know why,' the first man said. His skin was light, but his eyes were so dark they were like deep pools of space. Vacant, void, soulless. 'We need you to tell us where the mutt is.'

'Mutts! Dogs are man's best friend. There is no one here but me, good sirs. And maybe my dog.'

'Dog?'

'Yes.' I nodded and then stepped past my door so they could enter. 'I like to call him Sheriff Sparky, but he also does respond to good boy.'

Both men exchanged looks and then glanced at their devices. No doubt someone from Angie's had said something. Not Angie, the lovely lamb that she was, but maybe one of the other men I'd refused to help in years past. Even if no one could bring me up on crimes, didn't mean I didn't have enemies. 'Would you like to look around, boys?'

'Are you voluntarily allowing us to search your home?'

'Why not?' I said. 'I've nothing to hide.'

Both of them stepped into my front hall. They were about to take off their shoes when I stopped them. 'I don't recommend that. My dog's a little rough around the edges, and he will snap them up. He's the sheriff of this city, so you gotta respect the man, you know.'

'This dog.' The man in green narrowed his eyes at me and then looked around before adding, 'How long have you had him?'

'Time doesn't matter when you're with your best friend, and a man and his dog are timeless,' I said. 'But maybe two years? More like fourteen in dog years!'

I yammered on with all the dog platitudes I could think of, many of them from bad movies I'd seen on Earth, and eventually shut the front door behind the officers. I spoke loudly and clearly so that Jack could hear.

So that Jack could, in some way, save himself here.

'Is that the dog?' the man in green said. He walked into the living room without prompting and stopped when he was met with Jack on all fours. Without his clothing and with his back hunched like it was, he really did look like a dog. Those surgical transitions were amazing, and so was Jack's overall body language. He was like a big mastiff, a greyhound and a St. Bernard all rolled into one. His human form was present, but the way he'd shifted his body covered up the overtly human bone structure. It was like witnessing a before and after image reveal but without the gap. Jack was Jack; then, he was a dog.

'Whoa, boy,' the officer said. 'We mean no harm.'

'Sparky! Be polite to our guests.'

Jack sank back down into a more passive position, sniffed the couch and then went back to napping, his body folded around himself. He'd been naked since this started, but his fur and the careful movements meant I saw nothing of his genitals, or even his behind. That tail, though – that ever-present and never-wagging tail – hung off the back of the couch. Yet, even though it filled me with dread – that tail was the only thing Angie said could give away Caninites – I was still sure this plan would work.

'Well, let's let sleeping dogs lie,' I said and tried to stand in front of Jack's tail on the couch. 'Should we sit in my kitchen and have some coffee?'

'No thanks,' the officer in green said. 'But we do have some more questions.'

The three of us sat at my table, and they asked their questions. A lot of questions. I did my best to return just as rapid-fire, but my leg began to smart. Hard. The flesh and the wood never liked one another, but it was only as the emotional content of the conversation escalated, and my own crimes were hinted at, that I began to feel sick. Not just the queer feeling of lightheaded excitement – but nauseous. The pain was too much, and my body was too old, and it was quickly overwhelming.

Jack barked.

I stiffened. The officers jumped. 'It's okay,' I said, slowly realising what he'd done. 'I'm reaching the end of my ability to speak, though, gentlemen. My guide dog is getting a bit finicky, too.'

'Right, right,' the first officer said. 'We will get out of your hair. But tell me – if you have had this dog as long as you say, then what do you feed him?'

'He eats what I eat,' I said and turned the pain of my leg into rage. 'He's man's best friend, after all, and that's because he knows when I'm sick of bullshit like you guys barging in on my night and when I'm sick and just need to eat.'

Jack barked again. The clink-clink of his nails and genetically altered paws against the floor came closer, and soon enough, Jack was nudging open a cupboard in my kitchen as the officers watched mutely. There was food in there. He could smell it, and now we both desperately needed it. He took out a box of crackers and extended them to me. I took them, patted his head, and then encouraged him to sit at the table with me.

'But not you guys,' I said and stuffed a handful of crackers into my mouth. I slipped one or two down to Jack, who lapped them up off the floor. He also gnawed a bit at my wooden leg, but I figured I deserved that for making him grovel and beg with me. 'We're going to eat our bedtime snack and then go to bed because we're both old dogs here. I do hope you find who you're looking for.'

'Us too.' The man in green lingered, his eyes on Jack for an extra beat before he followed behind the first officer. 'Have a good night, Mr Brown.'

'Please,' I said. 'Call me Buck.'

'Buck,' they repeated in unison. When the man in green lingered and smiled, I was sure we were caught. So very sure. 'Good luck to your dog, sir. I hope he, too, feels better.'

'Better?' I repeated. I furrowed my brow. I'd said nothing about Sparky – or Jack – being sick. Then I remembered the tail. In spite of the great occasion of having two guests and Jack acting like a good boy to greet them, his tail did not wag.

He could not wag his tail.

That was the only thing he couldn't do as a dog.

'Oh, my love,' I said and ran a hand down Jack's back, over his carefully grafted fur and his spine to the lump of his tail. It was heavy in my hand, soft and yet bony. It was never going to move. But my grasping of it, my petting of my good boy, would propel some sort of glimmer over us.

I hoped.

'Poor thing. Yes, just a bit under the weather,' I said. 'Even more of a reason for us to settle into bed. I hope you have a good night, officers.'

Before anything could be said back, I rose from my chair, Jack behind me, and waddled over to the door. Shut it up tight. My leg smarted, it throbbed with pain and adrenaline, but nothing happened. I waited. Counted to three. Waited some more.

Jack stood on his hind legs again, tall like a man. He sniffed the air. 'They're gone. Can't smell 'em anymore. And I got a noseful. Ugh.' He turned around, giving himself some privacy as he put on his clothing once again. Just as his pants covered his waist, he huffed, grabbing his droopy tail that flopped out of them. 'I need to get this fixed. Is there a way to get this fixed now? They couldn't make it wag when I had the procedure, but maybe things have changed?'

'Hell if I know,' I said. I was focusing on a small patch of fur on his collarbone. I wanted to look at so many other places, but I kept my stare there. 'But that damn tail will be the death of us. You gotta cover it up.'

'Well, shit,' Jack said. 'Maybe I should just get the thing cut off. Be easier in some ways. What are those dogs that have their tails snipped?'

'Pinschers,' I said. 'But I should have known you were lying about being a free man. Dog. A freed prisoner.'

Jack winced. 'Sorry.'

'Sorry?'

'What?' Jack shrugged. 'I'm sorry I lied, but I'm a bit of an escapee right now. I just heard the news about Pete dying, and I knew something was up, so I left.'

'Just left,' I repeated, rolling my eyes. 'You make it sound so easy!'

'It is.' Jack shrugged and then bared his canine teeth in a grin. 'Why? You want to rub my nose in it? Hit me with a newspaper?'

My skin flushed, so I shook my head to cover it up. So much that I felt a little dizzy by the end. 'I really don't care if you're a dog or a man or a prisoner or a pirate or a freedom fighter. I really don't mind. Just that I should have known you were also an escapee. You should have told me the truth, but then again, I should have known you weren't going to.'

'What did you say?' Jack asked, a gleam in his eyes. 'Can't teach an old dog new tricks or something like that.'

'That's a really bad joke.'

'So is that other one you told. But I forgive you for the bad jokes if you forgive me for lying. Maybe now we can start off as something good and true.'

When Jack extended his hand, I almost didn't know what to do with it. His fingers were shorter, the calluses of paws marked his palm with pink and brown streaks. Yet it was such an obvious and open gesture. Our hands fit together so easily.

'Fair.'

'Fair,' I echoed. 'Now what?'

'Well,' Jack said, and both of us seemed to remember the diamond hiding in another room of my house. If those guys had searched a little harder, not been so fixated on finding a prisoner or analysing what I fed my dog, they might have spotted this glowing monstrosity instead. Two steps over, flip over a couple throw blankets, and huzzah. A diamond as big as my old camera that never worked anymore but I wanted to always keep.

'I still think people are after me,' Jack said after a moment. 'What I'd really like to do is ask you to fence this thing.'

'Me?'

'Yeah. You're still a fence, right? You think you can find a buyer for something like that without calling too much attention?'

'I think we have lost the ability to not call too much attention.'

'You know what I mean,' Jack said, and I actually did. He wasn't asking me to fence this; he was asking me to work with him. Fencing was only part of it, only the first problem in a myriad of other problems. Like being an escapee and probably, most definitely, being pursued by someone who actually did want him dead. And who probably wouldn't face any consequences if he did kill Jack because he was just a dogman.

'Damn dog,' I said, then huffed. Jack's ears perked up in anger I'd never seen before. 'Caninite,' I said. 'I'm sorry, I'll use the proper term.'

'No, you call me Jack.'

'Jack,' I said.

'Buck.'

We waited a moment longer, looking at one another, trying to figure out the next move. Handshake seemed too serious, too human. But I was in the dark about what else we could do to make our lives intersect in a way that wouldn't disrupt or irrevocably harm us both.

Jack turned away first. 'If you can't be a fence, maybe I can trade for something else? Because I need a ship. I have to keep moving so they don't find me. And if those goons don't find me, another person will. So I can't stay here for long, and though you've been kind, I really should—'

'That sounds... nice.'

'Nice? Jack laughed. 'Am I a good boy? This another bad joke?'

'No, I'm serious. It was a good life in the skies, you know. When I had it.'

'Even though people were after you?'

'Oh, sweetie, that was why it was fun.' I touched my chest, where my heart had been beating so fast tonight after remaining calm for so long. I wanted that life. I wanted more than the diamond, I understood now. I wanted Jack with me, my good boy or right-hand man, whatever was a better name for what the hell the two of us would become.

'What do you think,' I began, slowly forming the plan as I did, 'of us working together?'

~

'Well, I will be sad to see you leave,' Angie said. 'But all good boys must come to an end.'

'Hardy-har,' I said, but I was smiling right along with her. She plopped down two beers for me and Jack, plus our to-go order. A bowl was put down as well, completely optional. She chuckled as she placed the bag on the table. 'And here is your *doggie* bag. Isn't that cute?'

Jack narrowed his eyes at her, but it was all in good fun. If he could have, he would have wagged his tail. But I sort of liked it not wagging; it made my knowledge of what went on in his mind that much better, that much more intimate – as if the two of us could get any closer.

We'd found a buyer for the diamond quite happily, and when I suggested that we split the profits – it was my house, after all, and I hadn't even needed those keys to get inside it – and buy a ship together, Jack had agreed. 'Always so much better being a pirate when you have a sidekick,' he'd said, and I liked that I didn't know who was whose sidekick.

And pirate, anyway, was a slur.

Our vessel, the small but sturdy Little Sparky, was parked at the docks. I could see it from my regular spot at Haven, which would no longer be so regular. While Jack drank from his beer – in a glass – and nibbled on the peanut and pretzel snacks at the table, I stared out the window.

'You sad to go?' Jack asked. His drink was done. I'd barely touched mine.

I shook my head. I drank a swig and then made a face. 'Definitely not. Don't tell Angie, but I've never liked the drinks here. Food's not too bad, but I think we can find something better out there.'

I pointed to our ship, then past it, at the unknown mysteries before us. Jack slid a hand along my wooden leg, and with a nod of his head – one that sort of also wagged his tail – we left the bar together to head to our new home.

EVE MORTON

Eve Morton is a poet, professor, and parent living in Waterloo, Ontario. She likes coffee, short stories, and horror movies—in that order.

Event Horizon

Christina Ladd

THEY hang there like stars of flesh, limbs splayed into five haphazard directions like a child's idea of shining. And they are the lucky ones, though unlucky by their own philosophy. Damned, actually, or perhaps just in purgatory until another black hole chances by in a trillion years or so to suck them down to their heaven, their promised paradise.

Or perhaps their souls have done what their bodies could not and flitted the last distance into the supermassive. It has a name in their faith. She just can't remember what it is.

'Igul,' Captain Maimun says, as if in answer to her unasked question. He was here when she came to the viewport, and though she would prefer solitude, she cannot begrudge him the only unimpeded view of the starscape. It's his ship, after all. 'The circle that is the whole of creation.'

The black hole's actual designation is NGC 772704, but scores of people don't hurl themselves into mortal consummation with an alphanumeric string.

'That's right,' she says, reflexively professorial even though she has no real claim to it. She's still only a grad student. 'That's what they called it.'

If he registers her unintended pedantry, he doesn't comment. 'In the old days, they used to hang prisoners in cages,' he muses instead, and this morbid turn might be threatening if she could not see his glasses, his wristwatch. He is anachronistic, not violent. 'They would festoon the outer walls of their castles with their dead enemies.' And even though she knows that's not quite right, that the dead mostly adorned entryways and not whole castles, and then only in some far more specific times than simply 'old,' she likes the word *festoon* and rejects any impulse to correct him. Deep space makes poets or stoics of captains, and she would not like to push him toward the other extreme. 'As a warning,' he adds unnecessarily, or perhaps just non-specifically. *A warning against what?*

But she knows or can imagine. Castles of dark stone, flecks of mica and quartz glinting, as real and solid as the event horizon they are now skirting past. *Here be danger*, said the walls and the gibbets and the persistence of bones. *Here be dragons.*

In the 'old days,' they would write that on the edges of maps, but she thinks she has hit on a better truth: that the dragons have always been right in the centre, their gravity inescapable.

'Mm,' is all she says aloud, though. 'Crazy.'

The silence overtakes them like a dragon, too, rending their conversation to bits. It is hard to keep the threads out here, hard to think there's any point. Clarity of purpose is essential in space, mostly for captains and crew who must resist lassitude at all costs, but even passengers like her are drilled on acuity of intent. She passed all her tests very easily. No one was worried about a New Qarrawiyyin University scholar; everyone took for granted that an academic would be focused. She was not interrogated except to demonstrate her anthropological chops, and she dazzled them with citations until they signed off on her research.

She will never know now whether they would have approved the travel request if they had understood her history. They might well have been sympathetic. But half a lifetime of hiding has made her more cautious, not less, and what does it matter? She's here.

'*Is* it crazy?' Captain Maimun asks eventually.

'Yes and no,' she says blandly, the academic's favourite response, hiding the fact that she has lost all context for the conversation.

He nods. 'Crazy by whose terms?' he agrees, as if she's said something wise instead of hedging. 'They thought they would go through the black hole and end up in paradise. Tawhid – oneness. Singularity.'

'That's not what that means. The theology *or* the science.'

He nods. 'Drake was an ignorant man. Confident, though. Ignorance and confidence are a dangerous combination.'

'He called his charisma barakah. He said it was from God.' She uses her lecturing voice by mistake.

'They weren't Muslim,' Maimun says, contempt sharp, she thinks, from long honing. 'Ibrahim Drake was just Adam Drake in fancy dress. He changed his name to be more obviously foreign because 'Ādam wasn't exotic enough.'

'Sorry,' she says, truly contrite although it sounds reflexive. 'I'm sure you know all this better than I do.'

He inclines his head at her apology. Then he makes a rueful face. 'I doubt that. I forgot I was talking to a scholar and not a product management director. Or operations strategy consultant. Or whatever they call themselves now. The people who come this far out, they're bored and looking for entertainment. They think I must know gory details.'

'There are no gory details. Just sad ones.'

'Precisely.'

She's lying, though. The details are lurid, and she knows them by heart. She summons the attributes of sadness, the frown and slumped shoulders, the knit brow, the faraway look, not as an act but as a wish. She wants to feel sorry for each and every ugly fact – the boiling eyeballs and saliva, the ebullism mottling every bit of skin with bruises – but she doesn't. Because it's embolism or hypoxia that kills in space, and if those aren't painless, then at least they're quick. The brain, deprived of oxygen, slips off into night with muted fireworks and then the eternal nothing.

Her mother's life and death were similar in that regard: random bursts of brightness swallowed by an all-consuming dark.

It was the constant of her childhood, the sorrow that resisted all consolation. Even in memories where they are laughing, her mother's sadness asserts itself. *I have a hole in my heart*, her mother once said. To a five-year-old, this was literal and, therefore, comforting. Hearts and holes were known quantities. If neither she nor her mother could manage to fill it in, then surely a doctor would know what to do.

That – call it what it was – *faith* was misplaced. Her mother, in retrospect, had needed a philosopher, someone to acknowledge the existential conundrum of living and breathing in an environment not merely hostile but antithetical to life.

Instead, she went to psychologists, who called it *fernweh*, after the German word for far-sickness, longing for a place you had never been. One of them called it *Earthweh*, looking so pleased with herself for the portmanteau. She and all the others prescribed various antidepressants and, as an afterthought, time in the greenbanks. Plants arranged in dense towers for maximum efficiency, the term a nod to server banks, server farms – technology and biology approaching each other asymptotically. *Never to meet.*

She stares out at the event horizon and thinks of being so close and still so impossibly far.

The greenbank on Shutaitou Base was where Drake had found them. *Pain,* he'd said, *is not a mistake. It's holy.* It might have been the first time anyone had given her mother a purpose for her suffering instead of an explanation. No wonder she followed him: first from station to station, itinerant proselytiser, and then, when he became too much of a nuisance, from ship to ship, taking the worst jobs, the most dangerous.

No wonder her daughter had taken refuge in academia instead and lost herself in explanations. She did not want a purpose. Other students bemoaned the relative insignificance of their work; she took comfort from it. *No one will hurl themselves into the void because of me.*

Did her mother tumble past the event horizon? Or is she one of the orbiting corpses? It's impossible to tell; all of them wore the same suits, bulky things that obscured every trace of identity. Drake had liked that – at first. But then he could not tell one follower from another, or even the men from the women. And it was increasingly important that he be able to distinguish the women, more and more of whom he called his wives.

Male and female, he made them, she remembers Drake repeating, quoting the Qur'an as he brought in the red paint the station used to mark external fixtures. He told the women to paint their spacesuits with it. The children all around, helping, and she can still smell the reek of that toxic colour, like barely melted plastic.

She had been smearing designs along her mother's helmet, fourteen but a very young fourteen, sheltered, when Drake had ordered her to fetch her own suit. She went, unthinking. When she returned, it was to Drake standing over her mother, eyes boring into her head as she cast her gaze down, and him somehow both hissing and yelling *so which of your Lord's bounties do you both deny?*

He only quoted the Qur'an in English. He didn't know Arabic, and they were forbidden to learn lest they *misinterpret.*

The whole room was both looking and desperately not looking at the tableau, and she wanted to do the same, but her suit was heavy and bulky and eventually, one of the arms slipped out of her grasp, and the cuff thudded against the floor. The room turned to look at her. Drake turned to look at her.

Her childhood ended then, but only in retrospect. Only in retrospect do Drake's eyes gleam with lust, and only in retrospect does her mother's expression harden into resolution. Perhaps both those things happened, but the gravity of collective regard obliterated everything else, including memory.

She only knows that she painted her suit red, woman's red, on the outside long before she ever bled, and within three months, she had escaped. Or rather, she had *been escaped*, a passive construction that makes no sense when she tries to explain it but that she knows in her heart is true. Her mother took her hand and transferred it to a stranger's, a woman who did food resupply. They said nothing to one another or to her.

Space meant isolation. Space meant isolation was impossible.

She comes back to herself standing beside Captain Maimun, and the strange mixture of companionship and alienation gives her a sense of, if not contentment, then at least of rightness. Here is another stranger, one taking her toward instead of away.

Toward her mother, though he doesn't know it.

After she *was escaped*, she made no effort to contact her mother again. It's baffling to her now, but in a way that is confused rather than guilty. How could she not try? She doesn't know. It never occurred to her.

I was a child. The excuse is flimsy the way truth can often seem flimsy, less real than fiction, less monumental. *I didn't know.*

It was easier not to know. Easier to pretend that she was her uncle's daughter, her cousin's sister. Easier to let herself become a stranger because that was what her mother seemed to want. *She handed me to a stranger.* Under the anger, there was relief. Under the relief, there was anger, a never-ending ouroboros. A circle the size of creation.

Her mother gave her to a stranger because what she did not know was better than what she knew. And perhaps that's the uncloseable distance between them, not physical space or even life and death but the faith in the unknown.

It should have been the opposite. She owes her freedom, her life to the goodwill of strangers; if she can't muster a belief in fate, at least she should feel grateful for chance. For choices.

But her mother stayed. It's *that* unknowable choice that haunts her and not anything to do with herself. Her mother *stayed*, and she has never stopped needing to know why.

'Sad but infuriating too,' says the captain, and for a dizzy moment, she thinks it's the voice of God. She has lost the thread again. She wants to be back at the university, back planetside. Space seems to mean nothing but losing things.

'Hm?' she asks, abandoning further pretence that she is following along.

'Space is *vast*,' the captain says, and the word reverberates with lightyears. He knows better than most the meaning of the word. 'And Drake reduced it to a single black hole. He made his followers believe something so… small.'

She doesn't tell him that it wasn't like that, at least what she remembers. Drake told them that NGC 772704 was a gateway for the worthy, a passageway to the Garden. *When the stars have been extinguished*, he would quote and explain that a black hole was an extinguished star, an early site of God's judgment. *The Day of Decision is coming toward us, but we can also go toward it. And then Allah will reward us!*

Drake had not understood Islam any more than he understood astrophysics.

No one knows what happens inside a black hole. Oh, there are theories, but past the event horizon, the black hole is unobservable. Occluded.

Did her mother leap from the hatch, consumed by a desire to know, finally consumed by something other than her sorrow? Or had Drake obliterated everything inside her but obedience? Maybe that had been enough in itself: the negation of self, absence leaping with open arms toward absence.

'I think—'

The adhan sounds then, startling them both despite the gentle tone. Captain Maimun glances at his wrist, and she realises that she has misidentified the anachronism: it's not a watch but a qibla indicator, brasswork enclosing a four-dimensional display to point toward Earth, toward Mecca. There are apps for it, but its weight and intricacy are part of the point. It is a reminder that the universe has a direction.

Drake had hacked their indicators to point toward NGC 772704. The black hole obsession was only starting when she *was escaped*, but she remembers that much. That, and her mother's attentiveness to the new eschatology. Her eagerness for it.

Captain Maimun catches her looking, and they have an entire conversation with three raised eyebrows: one his, two hers. *Are you coming to prayers?* he invites, and she conveys a kind of rueful dismay: *Ah, if only.* If only – she could put aside her studies? If only – she could bring herself to believe? If only she were someone else entirely, in an entirely different place.

He does not inquire further, but when he reaches the door, he turns at the threshold.

'Will it help?' he asks, and there are so many things he means, but only one way she takes it.

'I don't know,' she admits.

He nods once, and then she's alone.

She wants so badly to feel the crushing loneliness of space, wants to hold her breath until despair spots her vision. But she can't. But she feels only the introvert's relief at having the viewport to herself, the grad student's perpetual undercurrent of guilt at not working.

Which means her mother is *gone*. Dead, of course, but now also *inaccessible*. When she was younger, missing her mother meant she felt connected to her. Her anguish was like a second heart, throbbing a metronome of living grief that made her mother's depression comprehensible. But her desire to understand became more and more academic over the years, and at this moment, facing down the void, she recognises that her sympathy has been entirely subsumed by her desire to *know*.

The black hole is there in the viewer. Thousands upon thousands of kilometres away, of course, the distance barely comprehensible on a human scale, but *present* in a way it never has been before in pictures. That, at least, does not disappoint her.

She came here wanting to know. Wondering if she could understand her mother, her mother's choices, which for a time determined her own and might still. But the black hole has claimed all, and no information escapes the event horizon.

After this, she will change the direction of her thesis. May even leave the subfield entirely, citing fatigue with the subject, or insufficient evidence, or just feigning a new obsession with something else.

It is essential that she come back in some way changed. This must have changed her. It must, instead of leaving her mirroring the nothing she sees through the porthole, a void where mother and daughter should be.

CHRISTINA LADD

Christina Ladd (she/her) is a writer, reviewer, and editor who lives in Minneapolis. She will eventually die crushed under a pile of books, but until then she survives on a concerning amount of tea and baked goods. You can find more of her fiction at christinaladd.com

THE ISLAND OF COLOURED FIELDS
Booker G.A. Feniks

'**MR** Gerhardt Teal. Your ship is ready.' The words were soft, spoken from the cracked lips of a hard-faced sailor. But it was the assumption of those words that made them sound the most cruel. Art received this news three nights after he contacted Captain Barthold Moe again. He wouldn't take up the offer for another three days.

He came from the Coloured Fields. Somewhere, out across the azure seas, his father once lived among the fields of wildflowers and fruit trees. Somewhere, amongst the crashing of waves, the wind sang as it danced through the stalks of anemones, begonias, carnations, sunflowers and more. Somewhere, beneath the white foam of bubbling lakes, his mother had been born. Somewhere, beyond the golden horizon lay Gerhardt's home, wreathed in a rainbow of fantastical flora.

Somewhere, on an island far away, Art had lost his heart thirty long years ago. Somewhere, it still waited for him, it still called out. Someday, he vowed he'd be back.

Someday, he longed to be back.

~

From the manuscript of Leon Robin Jr:
I met Gerhardt Jan Teal when he was exactly thirty years, five months and two days old. I was thirty-three then, more or less; I'm ashamed to say that I

hadn't kept as good a count as Art. He had come from across the seas in a ship whose sails tickled the skies, whose hull seemed to brush across the very bottom of the ocean. He was short, lean, fair-skinned, with a face few would call handsome. But he had this air about him; he had the peculiar talent of swaying even the coldest of crowds.

He dressed in all blue, this teal-ish colour that was closer to turquoise than to anything else. A purplish-pink pansy flower that sat with a bowed head within his suit pocket was the only pop of colour on his person. His hair had already turned silver, and he wore a curious pair of glasses upon his nose, with extra lenses and weird little levers sticking out of the main frame. His own work, he told me.

Art stayed on the Island of Coloured Fields for a week, sharing a cottage with my wife, Vivianne, and me. I never saw him again; I didn't expect to. And yet, every day for the next ten years, I went out onto the hill that overlooked the wharf where the Painted Lady had thrown down her anchor. And I waited and waited and looked across the horizon, hoping to once again see her sails tickling the skies.

I stopped visiting the hill twenty years ago, and yet, at heart… I'm still waiting.

Art told me of his fear of setting sail. He had never felt uncomfortable on a boat before; it was something else holding him back. It was the fear of nostalgia. Such powerful nostalgia, he was scared his heart would burst. Burst from the overwhelming love he felt for a homeland he knew very little about.

He told me this as we lay before the fireplace on the last day of his visit. His hair was shimmering in the light of the fire, and it was soft when I carded my fingers through it.

He said, 'Leon? Have you ever been to a place that you've always wanted to return to?' I shook my head, for I had never left the island before.

Art turned away from me, his pearly teeth biting down on his bottom lip as he thought. Art was a thinker; I was a doer. If he hadn't been overthinking his visit to the Coloured Fields, maybe he would have arrived years earlier. I'll never know now.

'Leon,' he said after a while, when I had put my head upon his shoulder and closed my eyes, 'I think I know how to explain this now.' I hummed in agreement and took his hand. His fingers were stained with chestnut ink, made from the ones we had gathered together earlier that day. He had callouses on his middle and pointer fingers and on his thumb, in the exact shape that he held a quill.

'If you wrapped a rope around your chest,' he began, and I felt the rumble of his words travelling from his body to mine where we were pressed together, 'tight enough for it to gently pinch the skin between the loops, and then if you pulled it… it would be but a fraction of the sensation I felt every time I thought about my homeland. My heart would speed up, and my throat would clench as if I was nervous of something. And there was always this pull, this *yearning,* that I could never shake. Am I making any sense, Leo?'

'All the sense in the world, my love.' I remember his lips pressing against my hairline, and they were lightly cracked from all the time we had spent outside, bathed by the salty wind of the sea. If I concentrate hard enough, I think I can still feel the sensation of his lips on my skin.

&

On the day Art arrived, I was talking to Vivianne. It was the same conversation again.

'We can't stay here forever, Leon.' She was in her yellowish-beige sweater, in the colour we called bisque. I wore a shirt in a similar shade, with a robin feather in my hair. Red was my colour, it always had been, the crimson shade of a male robin's breast. Vivianne had a button on her sweater that was purple, periwinkle exactly. We were Mr and Mrs Bisque in name only, but I was Leon Robin, she was Vivianne Periwinkle, and there was no love between us.

'And go where, Vivianne?' I can't remember how many times we had that conversation before Art came and how many more times she brought it up after he left.

'Anywhere.' She said that every time. 'The world is such a vast place!'

'We've never been off the Island before.' I said that every time.

'So? We could always learn to live in other places, just like we learned to live here!' Every time she said that, I felt the urge to grab her by the shoulders, to sit her down and explain to her that I didn't want to leave. I wanted her to understand the love I felt for the Island. I wanted her to know of the pride that burst from my heart when I looked upon the Fields, the joy I felt every season when the fruit trees bloomed. I wanted her to understand not just my reservations about living in a new, different place. I wanted her to finally understand that this was where I was happiest.

She could never understand my happiness, and I couldn't fault her for it. She could never find joy here.

I didn't have the time to reply, although all my replies were always the same: 'Maybe someday.' My 'maybe' was cut off by a yell and a stampede of feet coming from the beach.

'Ships!'

'Outsiders!'

'Guests!'

I could hardly understand what the people were saying, which yell was coming from whom. I couldn't even tell who, in the monochrome mass of people, was actually talking; at some point, all the townsfolk blended into one.

It was Vivianne who finally got me to move. I was content to stay where I was, in the dip between the hill where our stout little cottage sat and the plane of houses that made up the rest of our quaint village.

To this day, I cannot say if I'm happy or angry that Captain Barthold Moe of the Painted Lady chose our western bank over the eastern, southern, or northern ones.

If he hadn't, I never would have met Art Teal. I never would have waded through the water, my shoes left somewhere on the road, my trousers bunched up at the knees. I never would have helped Gerhardt out of the little rowboat, tripping and twisting my ankle as we both fell back into the waves. I never would have heard his baritone voice chime out a laugh as he complained about his wet teal suit. I never would have fallen in love.

To this day, I don't know if I should be happy about it.

∿

'I *am* so sorry, sir!' Gerhardt wasn't very handsome. He had a small nose that disappeared into the rest of his face. He had small, squinty eyes that were a mundane shade of grey. His mouth was a thin, straight line trembling just slightly above his rounded chin, and the moustache he wore felt wholly out of place on his round, boyish face. It was his laugh that I fell in love with, and then his voice. His voice was deep, a rich baritone; I can still hear it today. He had an accent that intrigued me; he stretched out his vowels and trilled out his consonants, and when he said my name, I felt as if I was floating. He said it Leh-on, instead of Lee-ohn like everyone else on the Island, like even Vivianne said it.

I was in no place to reply then, as he was pulled up and off me by Barthold. It wasn't the eccentric hissing on the esses or the emphasis he put on the 'am' instead of the 'so' that distracted me from a reply. 'Fuckin' hell!' It was the pain from my ankle that had me shouting into the sky. I called on every god I knew of and on the ones I didn't know, cursing them all as the pain pulsed through my entire leg.

I must have passed out at some point. I remember Jeremiah and Olson, the Ink brothers, carrying me between them. I remember a flash of Vivianne's pretty, worried face looking right at me. I remember the pain that shot through me, from my ankle up to my very throat, when Franz White, the village doctor, was checking on me. And then, I remember the weight of a blanket, and the warmth of a fire, and nothingness.

When I came to, my ankle was stiff but pain-free. The blanket I was covered in was red; it was the one my mother had made for me when I was a child. I was at an age, back then, such that the blanket still fits me today, more or less, and yet young enough for no one to wonder why I had colours on me.

And then, then there was Art. He sat on the chair before the fire in our cottage in only his undershirt. The shirt, like the rest of his garb, was blue. In his fingers, he held the pink pansy, gazing down upon it with a soft smile. The fire illuminated his face, the wrinkles and the laugh lines, and I felt my heart skip a beat.

'Where did you get that flower?'

Art jumped, almost dropping the precious thing onto the floor. His startled expression reminded me of a baby cow, surprised that it had fallen over.

'I have it from home.' His voice, although quiet, sent a shiver through me. 'It's the colour my mother, Elke Orchid, wore. I inherited my colour after my father, Frederich Teal, but I still wear something of my mother in her honour.' He had puffed out his chest, and the smile he now wore was proud; I would almost call it patriotic.

It took me a moment to realise what he meant about the colours and his parents. I didn't even know his name, but I was already in love with my Art.

'Here, you lost this when you helped me out of the rowboat.' His fingers were uncharacteristically clumsy, then, when he pressed and poked at the pockets of his trousers. He fumbled with the item he wanted to give me, and when he finally did, I was presented with a slightly damp, slightly squished robin feather.

I don't remember our first kiss very well. I just know that it happened when he was braiding the feather into the braid at the nape of my neck. I remember it being sweet, chaste, and that his lips chased after mine afterwards. I think we might have spent the rest of the day kissing because when I woke up again, Art was gone.

Instead, Vivianne sat before me. She was smiling. She knew.

&

I had a sister once. Sara Robin, my twin sister, our father's favourite. She taught me how to braid my hair when we were five, as she had always been the faster learner.

She had brown hair, dark like the seeds of an unpicked sunflower. Vivianne was always a blonde, straw-yellow. The village folk called them the Sunflower Twins because of how well they complimented each other and the way they would spend their whole days playing amongst the sunflowers. I was the only person who knew what sort of games they really played, hearing every night the tales of Sara's explorations as we lay together beneath the red blanket mother had made me.

Sara was bold, brash, loud. She was inquisitive and hated being ignored. She left the Island when she was of age; Vivianne was inconsolable for days. I sat with her and held her, and she cried into my shoulder, fat tears that weren't for me to see. But I was the closest thing she had to Sara.

A year after Sara left, Vivianne turned of age. We were married three months later.

Exactly a year to the day when Art left, Vivianne followed him. Before she went, she got up onto her tiptoes and pressed a petal-soft kiss to my temple. Her gentle voice reverberated in my ears, even though she only whispered. She told me how she and my sister had promised each other something before Sara left.

I never saw Vivianne again, just like I never saw Sara again. I can only hope they found each other. I can only hope they are happy.

No one can remember the day the Grey family moved into our little western village. Some say the patriarch of the family was called Phillip Grey, and he came from overseas, but no one remembers him anymore. It often seemed that, for as long as the village existed, so had the Greys, watching over us from their cottage at the tree line.

Alphonso Grey was the newest alderman in the village. He was a lanky, thin, crooked-backed man.

He wore, as his name suggested, all grey, but his hair was also grey, as were his eyes. His skin was a sickly shade but grey as well, and the handlebar moustache he wore always reminded my sister of a fat, grey rat.

As a child, I thought Grey was someone I should look up to. He had a wife, he had children, he watched over the village, and everyone said he was a just and dignified alderman, an intelligent man who could solve any issue set before him. It was only after my sister left that I realised no one really knew Alphonso Grey. That the exterior of the benevolent alderman hid beneath it the carapace of a cruel, cold man just waiting to reveal itself, waiting to burst from beneath his skin like a worm bursting from beneath the skin of a rotten apple.

Grey came to my and Vivianne's cottage when my wife was tending to me. For all the love that didn't exist between us, there existed a bond of friendship that meant far more to the both of us. She was feeding me soup, as the pain made me weak, when Grey stepped into the cottage, Mr White coming in behind him.

Franz, an old friend of my mother's, wore a small slip of cloth in his pocket, the colour of a raw, cut-open peach. I think it was a handkerchief once, the sort that the women in the village wore around their heads, but I could never be sure. I never got the chance to ask him.

'Mrs Bisque, where is Mr Teal?' Grey had a scratchy, raw voice. The complete opposite of the voice that responded.

'Here I am.' I craned my head to look at him as Art came out of the nearby door.

Grey's face was twisted into an expression that terrifies me to this day, and when he spoke, it sent a shiver through my body that I could never forget. 'Mr Teal. I hope I am not interrupting. I've come here to ask you how fast you are planning to leave.' Grey paused, and Art opened his mouth to reply, but Grey didn't let him, 'You see, Mr Teal, you may have been born here, as were your parents, but we have some rules here that you have failed to follow. You, with your bright blue dress, spit in the face of all the workers that live on the Island of Coloured Fields. Our famed Fields produce flowers of unimaginable colours, but as you see, we do not use them. We do not taint them; we do not murder them to satisfy our own whims. We, here on the Island, work tirelessly to uphold the beauty of this land and, alongside it, the values that we have held very dear for generations. We do not want some Continental drifter here, spreading lies and falsehoods, influencing our children, manipulating them into believing that using colours as an adult is a good and moral thing to do. We do not want your Continental ideals poisoning the minds of our people! Am I making myself clear?' When Grey was done spitting and hissing at him, Art nodded silently and sat down in the chair left by Vivianne.

Vivianne, like my sister, was always a bit brash, and Grey's outburst had her jumping out of her seat. She didn't, however, dare stand up to him, not until the very day of her leaving the Island.

Alphonso Grey is gone now, and his son (once the oldest of the Grey girls) has turned out to be a far better man than his father ever was. And yet, every time I look into his grey face, I see in his eyes his father, and I still shudder.

❧

It was on the third day of his stay that I took Art to the Coloured Fields.

We climbed up an incline, his arms around my waist steadying me as I hobbled ahead with my leg in a splint. My arms were around his shoulders, tracing over his biceps and the skin of his neck and collarbones. I was a head taller, but he didn't lack the strength to carry me where I wished.

He was laughing as I pulled him along, tearing through the trees around us. He was adorably clumsy, and each branch that gently bounced off him made him laugh harder until we had to stop for him to catch his breath. That was when we had reached the top, and I hovered my hand over a branch blocking our view, ready to push it aside.

Art always squinted when he laughed, and the harder he laughed, the harder he squinted. When he finally opened his eyes, his laughter caught in his throat. I watched him as he took a step forward, and the light of the midday sun lit up his face as if he were one of its lost rays, fallen to the earth.

There, below us, were the Fields. Sectioned off based on colour, the work of countless generations, were the sprawling Coloured Fields. The horizon seemed endless, an empty blue sky that melted perfectly into the sea of purple petals. The gradient followed on from there, from purples to pinks to reds, then oranges and yellows, ending at a multitude of shades of green beneath our feet. And on either side lay the flowers that were brown and black and white, and colours that I have no words for. There were asters and honeysuckles, chrysanthemums and baby's breaths, and so many roses of so many colours that I wouldn't know where to start listing them all.

And amongst those flowers, the most beautiful thing I saw was Art and only Art. He had this small, quaint smile on his lips, as if he was remembering something, and the smell of the Fields was so intoxicating that I just couldn't help myself. Art was a thinker; I was a doer. So, I kissed him. I might have blacked out again, but I think we made love.

It sounds so silly in retrospect. Making love as we lay entwined together on a hill overlooking the Fields. I lied about blacking out. I remember every second of it as if it had just happened. The smell of the flowers was like an aphrodisiac, and when he shed his clothes, it reminded me of a flower escaping from its bud. The taste of his body was like the honey the bees cultivated from the flowers, and the touch of his skin was soft and pliable. It reminded me of the stories my sister would tell me, of her and Vivianne loving each other between the sunflowers when they were young. It sounded silly to me then; it sounds silly to me now.

I can't help but love it.

❧

It has been, if I have counted correctly, thirty-four years. To the day. Today, thirty-four years ago, Gerhardt left me, left the Island of Coloured Fields, never to return. I still remember the gleeful look Grey had at the time. Barthold, the hard-faced sailor with a soft voice, looked at us with contempt. What was he thinking in that moment? That we were rejecting Gerhardt, his friend? That we, his kinsmen, his family, didn't want him because of something as silly as colour? As a single, simple difference between him and us?

Vivianne wasn't there when Art left, and I couldn't blame her then. I still can't. I barely attended myself. I barely…

I don't think I can put into words that day. Art left his heart on the Island then, never to return. Maybe, like before his arrival, he longs for it still. Maybe. I don't know. All I know is that…

~

Leon was pulled away from his desk by the sounds of yelling. Yelling? It sounded more like a cheer that rose up through the whole village. He couldn't remember the last time the village folk were so rowdy, so happy and excited.

He grabbed his cane and threw his braid over his shoulder. Years later, he still couldn't shake the habit of braiding a robin feather into it. He wiped his glasses on the soft cotton of his robin-red shirt and hobbled out of his cottage, the one he once had shared with Vivianne.

Leon didn't know what he was seeing at first. Tall masts that tickled the skies and a hull with a young woman on the front. And a man, waving from the deck. And the Fields smelled deliciously that day, as the wind carried their smell towards the sea.

Leon ran, and somewhere along the road, he lost his shoes and his cane. Somewhere along the way, he bunched his red trousers up to his knees, and he dove into the foaming waters of the wharf. Somewhere along the way, he felt like a young man again, and on the deck, he saw small, squinty eyes looking at him from behind curious, mechanical glasses.

There was a moment, a single moment, where Leon thought he wouldn't catch him. But Gerhardt was as light as ever, and his head fit so perfectly against the crook of Leon's neck. He smelled like ink and pansies. And when he laughed, it was like a chime in the darkness.

'I missed you,' Art whispered into his ear. 'My heart.'

BOOKER G.A. FENIKS

Booker-Garet August Feniks (Booker G. A Feniks) is a queer, disabled writer of fantasy, comedy, and poetry. He writes stories that pull directly from their experiences growing up trans and autistic in a foreign country. Originally from Poland, Kielce, Booker writes primarily in English, and has a passion for linguistics and storytelling as a whole. He is young, ambitious, and optimistic about the changing future, although not unfamiliar with activism and the more difficult aspects of growing up marginalised.
You can find him on his website

https://upinflamesstories.wordpress.com and on their tumblr https://www.tumblr.com/up-in-flames-writing.

ABOUT THE PUBLISHER

A Coup of Owls Press was formed in early 2021 before publishing our first issue in June 2021. Initially bi-monthly, we now publish a quarterly online issue of eclectic and diverse short fiction that is free to read online or download. We only publish creators from underrepresented and/or marginalised communities or backgrounds. We are a Coup rather than a Parliament. We always strive to embrace the other and the different, and want to lift all those living in other worlds.

AVAILABLE FROM A COUP OF OWLS PRESS

Other & Different (2023 anthology)
Other Worlds (2024 anthology)

Quarterly online short fiction
available to read and download free at:
www.acoupofowls.com

Dedicated to everyone living in

www.ingramcontent.com/pod-product-compliance
Lightning Source LLC
Chambersburg PA
CBHW061213210726
48294CB00006B/1829